SIDDHARTHA

Born in Calw in 1877, Hesse was the son of a family of Protestant clergymen and missionaries. He rebelled against his stern classical education in Swabian monastery schools, and worked as a locksmith and a bookseller before the success of his early poetry and prose made a writing career possible. Hesse wrote throughout sixty-five years and was awarded the Nobel Prize for Literature in 1946. He settled in Switzerland in 1911, after travelling as far as India, the land he considered his spiritual home. His pacifism and opposition to German militarism made him unpopular during the First World War and he was later condemned by the Nazis, yet Hesse remains one of the great literary figures of the German-speaking world. His novels, such as *Der Steppenwolf* and *Siddhartha*, and his critical writings have won him a place among leading contemporary thinkers. Hermann Hesse died in 1962, just after his eighty-fifth birthday.

Also by Hermann Hesse in Picador

THE GLASS BEAD GAME

DEMIAN

THE JOURNEY TO THE EAST

Hermann Hesse

SIDDHARTHA

Translated from the German by
Hilda Rosner

With an introduction by
Donald McCrory

PICADOR

First British Commonwealth edition published 1954 by Peter Owen Limited

This edition published 1998 by Picador
an imprint of Macmillan Publishers Ltd
25 Eccleston Place, London SW1W 9NF
Basingstoke and Oxford
Associated companies throughout the world
www.macmillan.co.uk

By arrangement with Peter Owen Ltd

ISBN 0 330 35485 X

7 9 8 6

A CIP catalogue record for this book is available from
the British Library.

Typeset by Intype London Ltd
Printed and bound in Great Britain by
Mackays of Chatham plc, Chatham, Kent

Contents

Preface to Siddhartha

This edition of *Siddhartha* includes biographical details of Hermann Hesse as well as an interpretation of the novel. Given that Hesse considered art and life as one, I have sought to show how a series of influential experiences, together with his encyclopaedic readings, weave their way into the novel.

Hesse's intense studies of Eastern and Western philosophical and spiritual works, in particular the *Upanishads* and the *Bhagavad Gita* and the works of Goethe, Nietzsche and Schopenhauer, account for a great deal of what we read in *Siddhartha*. Although the works of other major writers such as Novalis, Burckhardt and Freud come into the reckoning, I have attempted to trace those which have most bearing on the novel's contents, in order to appreciate – in all its wonder – a favourite work of Hesse's which, since publication in 1922, has had an astonishingly wide and diverse readership.

So much has been written about Hesse, in the USA, Japan, India, Germany and other parts of Europe, that access to the scholarship available is by no means simple. Hesse himself wrote so much – novels, tales, fairy stories, poems, personal letters, as well as countless reviews for several leading newspapers – that he helped to create a minor industry of critics and researchers, culminating in the periodic international conference held in Calw, devoted exclusively to all things Hessean. To keep abreast of such activity is almost a full-time job.

Detailed studies of his major works are now in print as well as numerous articles on all aspects of his voluminous output. His collected works, re-published in paperback in 1987 by Suhrkamp, run to several volumes.

Authors come into and go out of fashion and there is no doubt that Hesse was the 'man to be reading' in the 1960s and 1970s. Together with *Steppenwolf*, *Siddhartha* was everybody's guide to the galaxies of ancient India and beyond. However, Hesse still has something useful to say to today's world. The message or meaning of *Siddhartha* – and it will vary from reader to reader – is as valid as ever.

The task of interpreting *Siddhartha* is made doubly difficult in that Hesse said and wrote (normally in reply to readers' letters) a fair amount about the text at different stages in his career. He did not quite contradict himself, but would emphasize certain aspects at one time and others another. Aware of this, I have tried to assimilate the 'constants' in Hesse's views – after all, he was to live another forty years – and weld them to the 'findings' of the growing number of Hesseanists.

What can prove a problem for both reader and student is Hesse's use of basic tenets from Eastern philosophy, an area beyond the ken of most modern readers. I have tried to elucidate those aspects of ancient Indian thought and belief that are integral to the novel and thus to our appreciation and understanding of it. The reader will find, in the list of Sanskrit and Buddhist terms provided, an indication of possible meanings and/or definitions relevant to their context. I have also added a list of the more important people mentioned in the Introduction, as an interesting aspect of Hesse's life is the rich contact he enjoyed with the intelligentsia of his day.

In the Introduction all translations from the German and Sanskrit are mine, as are the interpretations of the novel and explanations of Vedantic philosophy which underpin it. I have tried to render, in today's language, what I believe Hesse was attempting to convey.

No one can write anything of value about the life and works of Hesse without being indebted to the efforts of several scholars in the field. I should like to mention in particular the work of Joseph Mileck, the critic who has done most to promote, in the English-speaking world, all things Hessean, and to both Christian Immo Schneider and Fritz Böttger, whose studies of Hesse, in German, were among the best I discovered.

Donald McCrory

HERMANN HESSE (1877–1962): BIOGRAPHICAL DETAILS

Hermann Hesse was born on 2 July, 1877 in the little town of Calw on the edge of the Black Forest. His family background was unusually varied. His father was Johannes Hesse, a devout Pietist* priest who had spent four years (1869–73) in India as a missionary, but on account of ill health was forced to return home where he found work with Hermann Gundert, director at that time of the Basle Mission Society Publishing House. It was while working here that Johannes met and married Gundert's daughter, Marie. She had been born in India in 1842, educated in Germany and Switzerland and until 1870 had continually shuttled between the sub-continent and Europe. Her father, also named Hermann, had spent some thirty years as a missionary in India, spoke several Indian languages and had dedicated himself to the study of all things Indian. It was into this 'exotic' yet deeply Christian household that the author of the novel *Siddhartha* was born.

As his parents intended that he should follow in the footsteps of his maternal grandfather and father, the young Hermann was sent to Maulbronn, one of the four exclusive Protestant church-schools in Wurttemberg. Having passed the notoriously difficult Swabian state examination, his future seemed assured. Indeed,

Pietist: Followers of Pietism, a somewhat strict and, for Hesse, drab movement within the Lutheran Church. It stressed inward and practical religion, and 'supported' religious tolerance, but its narrow moral attitudes irked young Hesse.

his early letters to his parents suggest that he was more than happy with his new surroundings, his studies, his teachers and fellow-pupils. His enjoyment, however, was shortlived for in March 1892 he ran away from the school and disappeared for some twenty-three hours. This act of rebellion, inexplicable to both parents and teachers, began a series of crises that was to shatter all notion of a formal education and destroy the family's hopes of a career for Hermann in the Church.

Two months later, much to the relief of the school authorities, he was hastily withdrawn from the school and taken to Pastor Christoph Blumhardt of Bad Boll for a 'cure'. His behaviour had cast doubts upon his sanity. Although young Hesse suffered from headaches and insomnia, he seemed quite contented in his new 'home' until unrequited love for a vicar's daughter, named Eugenie Kolb, seven years his senior, threw him into a deep depression. He borrowed money, bought a revolver and on 20 June he disappeared, leaving behind a suicide note. He reappeared that same day, no doubt to the immediate relief of Blumhardt who, two days later, placed Hesse in the care of another priest, Pastor Schall of nearby Stetten. Good behaviour prompted Schall to allow the young recalcitrant to return home. In Calw, however, he rapidly became unsettled and was sent back to Schall's school which, it should be noted, was designed for 'mentally retarded and emotionally disturbed children'. His parents were clearly at their wits' end.

Hesse had become a rebel – but a rebel with a

cause – and for the remainder of his life he would uphold the rights of the individual against authority, crass materialism and the decline of culture. Sadly but all too rapidly, he realized that he was an 'outsider', and would have to find his own way in the world. As a result his novels record what became the highly individual 'inner' journey of a man who sought to discover his 'true' self. From an early age he felt impelled to nurture the needs of his soul as well as his discernible talents. Doing anything else, following another route, would lead him away from his self-imposed ideal of listening to the voice within. How else, he would argue, could he remain true to himself?

In letters to his parents written from Pastor Schall's school in Stetten, Hesse inveighs against the establishment, his father, adult authority and formal religion. The letters show him to be a seething, belligerent pupil who would not submit to the stultifying practices that surrounded him. The reader of German is urged to study his early outpourings and to juxtapose them with the novels written before 1922; in particular, with *Unter Dem Rad* (*Beneath the Wheel*) (1904), *Demian* (1919) and *Klingsor's Letzter Sommer* (*Klingsor's Last Summer*) (1920).

Nevertheless, for readers of *Siddhartha* (1922) who are unfamiliar with Hesse's other writings, the nature and intensity of his outbursts may come as a deep surprise. The pain, anger and frustration contrast so vividly with the joy, equanimity and gradual acceptance of life's flow which he describes so touchingly in his

Indic poem. The source of his vehemence is what he deems to be blatant parental rejection.

'What wouldn't I give for death! ... A miserable 1892! It began dismally in the seminary, a few blissful weeks in Boll, then disappointed love, and an abrupt end! And now – I've lost everything: home, parents, love, belief, hope, and myself ... Stetten is hell for me ... I'm going to be cold, ice-cold towards everyone, everyone! ... Goodbye, goodbye, I want to be alone ... Let me, the mad dog, die here, or be my parents!' (1 September, 1892)

' ... I don't deserve this. I love myself, just as everyone loves himself, but that isn't why I can't live here, rather it's because I need a different atmosphere to want, and be able, to fulfil myself as a human being,. . . . Here there's no hope and belief, no one loves or is loved; it's quite devoid of any ideal, of anything beautiful, anything aesthetic; there's no art here, no feeling ... no spirit ... I'm a human being and before nature I insist earnestly and solemnly upon the universal right of man ... I'm a human being, as Jesus was; I see the difference between the ideal and life as it is as well as he did, but I, I'm not as tough as the Jew.' (11 September, 1892)

To an extraordinary degree these brief extracts reveal issues and attitudes that were to become hallmarks of Hesse's prose; the yearning for acceptance, the belief in an ideal, the conflict between spirit and the flesh, the upholding of the dignity and value of the individual. Above all else, there rises the intense longing for physical and spiritual self-fulfilment, but not of the kind envisaged by his family. This longing that became his life-long quest gave rise to the unmistakable spiritual quality of his writings. It surfaces here, for when Hesse wrote these impassioned lines he knew he was destined for the priesthood.

The problems that erupted at fifteen had first been detected in 1881, when Hesse was still a child. In a letter to her husband, hard-pressed Marie complains that Hermann '... is unusually lively, extremely self-willed, and has quite an amazing understanding for a four-year-old ... God must take this proud spirit in hand; something noble and splendid will then come of it. But I shudder to think of what could become of this passionate human if subjected to a wrong or weak upbringing.'

Hesse's wish to follow his own path began very early and this caused his mother untold nightmares. Mentally he was very strong, but not so physically; headaches, insomnia, nervous tension and bouts of depression undermined his well-being from early childhood onwards, ailments exacerbated in later years by gout, sciatica and chronic eye-strain. Her admission that a 'wrong or weak upbringing' could cause untold harm is interesting, as it could be argued that, in their desire to channel Hesse's talents and energies, his parents created the very conditions that led to his vitriolic attacks.

Given that Hesse was a hyper-sensitive, hyper-active and headstrong child, it is not difficult to see how overbearing parental control, no matter how well-intentioned, could have triggered off in him exactly what they were trying to prevent. Coupled to home pressures (Hesse may well have called them oppressions), the school system in Wilhelmine Germany did nothing to alleviate matters. In fact the severely regimented schoolday, described so well in Hesse's second novel, *Unter Dem Rad* (*Beneath the Wheel*) published in 1904, lies at the root of the truancy and tragic death – it may well have been suicide – of the protagonist, young Hans Giebenrath, a thinly disguised Hermann Hesse.

By November, the young rebel had resumed his studies in a secondary school in Cannstadt. But there was no real improvement. He was unable to study, became depressed and again flirted with thoughts of suicide. Overwhelmed by his personal circumstances, he resorted to the life of a social misfit. He frequented pubs, smoked heavily, mixed with undesirables, incurred debts and virtually forced his parents to withdraw him from school. Reluctantly, they allowed him to return home where, after a few false starts (he spent fifteen grimy months in Calw as an apprentice machinist), he began an apprenticeship in a bookshop in Tübingen that lasted four years (1895–99). He had found his feet.

Although school had not been a success for Hesse, he had shown a marked interest in literature, especially in German literature of the eighteenth and nineteenth centuries. In Tübingen he continued his prodigious reading and autodidactism and in 1899 had his first book published, a collection of poems entitled *Romantische Lieder* (*Romantic Songs*). More significant, however, was his first prose publication which he called *Eine Stunde hinter Mitternacht* (*An Hour after Midnight*) which was reviewed somewhat sympathetically by Rilke, who described it as ' ... honest and deep, his love grand and its feelings are pious. The work stands at the edge of art.'

To an idealistic and talented 22-year-old this was praise indeed. The response of his parents, however, could not have been more negative. They implored their son to abandon writing. His mother in particular, appalled at the Romanticism of his work, wrote a letter pleading with him to flee his impure muse. Needless to say, Hesse was too headstrong to be dissuaded. Their remarks left him with deep scars. He never forgot his mother's letter and was never quite able to forgive his parents.

In the summer of 1899, Hermann moved to Basle to work as an assistant bookseller. He spent five fruitful years here during which he wrote more poetry, undertook two trips to Italy and, in 1903, finished his first novel, *Peter Camenzind*. In that same year he married Maria Bernoulli, nine years his senior. He then gave up his job to become a full-time writer and moved to Gaienhofen. Here, Hesse began a journey in which his life was his art and his art was his life. He was to produce a series of novels that would bring him both praise and derision, culminating in the Nobel Prize for

Literature awarded in 1946, some twenty-four years after the publication of *Siddhartha*.

GAIENHOFEN (1904–1912)

These are mixed years for Hesse. He continued his 'education' by reading widely, in particular Latin, Middle High German and Italian Renaissance literature, and maintained his very strong interest in German Romantic writers, especially Novalis. While he also appreciated his fellow contemporary writers, he preferred to associate with artists and composers. Indeed, many of the major characters of his tales and novels are painters and musicians. To this general rule *Siddhartha* is a notable exception.

Yet despite his growing interests, good income and promising future, life in Gaienhofen was proving rather irksome. Joseph Mileck explains in his biography of Hesse that he 'resented the loss of his bachelor's freedom' and, in order to make a distressing situation as bearable as possible, 'he yielded to his urge to roam'. There is no doubt that Hesse travelled more during these years than in any other period of his long and extremely active life, despite poor health.

Whatever the reasons for Hesse's disenchantment with married life, there is no denying the fact that his enormous workload must have imposed an unbearable strain on his wife Marie. Although she had borne him three children, Bruno in 1905, Heiner in 1909 and Martin in 1911, she took a poor second place to her husband's literary pursuits. How could any wife live with a man – no matter how gifted – who believed that he had given up too much for too little? As strong-willed as Hesse, she was equally set in her ways, and showed as little interest in his writings as he did in their domestic life. Gradually they drifted apart. Hermann devoted himself to his writing, his circle of painters and musicians and to gardening, whilst Maria tied herself more to her children, her home and her love of singing. They were eventually divorced in 1923, long after the marriage had failed.

The increasing literary output of Hesse during this period (1904–12) explains, at least in part, the growing isolation felt by Maria. Not only was Hesse writing new and significant material (collections of tales, legends, novels), but also poetry, nature sketches, travel reports, literary essays, and several translations from Latin (Ovid), French (Verlaine) and Shakespeare's *Romeo and Juliet*, many of which were published. In addition, he wrote much that was not. Like many writers and intel-lectuals of his day, he was a prolific letter-writer; his personal correspondence fills several volumes.

Enormous mental energy and time went into his pub-lications – after all, he had to make a living – but his self-imposed demands left little time for any family life. Then he decided to accept work as a reviewer and editor. The most onerous undertaking was his work as a book reviewer for the *Neue Zürcher Zeitung*, which he began in 1903 and continued, albeit with regular lapses, throughout his adult life. Furthermore, he became a staff reviewer for a subsidiary newspaper of the *Münchener Zeitung*; his contributions appeared from 1904 to 1917 and from 1930 to 1934. Indeed, from 1904 to 1912 articles by him appeared in at least eleven other newspapers and magazines. The first collection of Hesse's reviews, published in 1910, contained more than three thousand pieces.

We can but admire the energy, enthusiasm and intellectual appetite of this lonely but remarkable individual. Lonely, because to achieve what he achieved necessitated the life of a semi-recluse; remarkable, because the cultural impact of his writings, in particular of his reviews, spanning some sixty-three years in more than fifty of the better-known periodicals and newspapers of German-speaking Europe, must have been considerable. Review work meant that he had to read, digest and comment on an enormous body of work, and thus he was able to continue his self-education. A survey of his review writing reveals a man who had his finger on the pulse of contemporary German writing, but whose interests spread to world literature past and present, to art, religion, history, philosophy, psychology and, importantly for an understanding of Siddhartha, to the cultures and spiritual wisdom of the East.

His reviews of the works of the Sanskritist scholar, Garbe, of the Indologist Deussen (whose translations of the *Upanishads* Hesse read and studied avidly), of Neumann, whose translations of Buddha's *Talks* were published in 1921, and of the works of Richard Wilhelm, perhaps the greatest German scholar of

13

ancient Chinese texts, are of particular relevance to the thematic content of the novel. As a reviewer, Hesse repeatedly declared that he would only draw attention to those texts he believed would 'survive'. Without these translations, Hesse would not have been able to steep himself in the sacred writings of the East, a self-imposed task that he had to fulfil in order to study, reflect on and eventually to 'live' Eastern philosophical writings.

Among the many influential writers and thinkers that Hesse read and admired, there are three that deserve special mention here, for all three have a bearing on the finished version of *Siddhartha*: Nietzsche, Schopenhauer and Jacob Burckhardt, the historian who replaced Nietzsche as the guiding light in the second half of Hesse's life. Hesse had read the major works of all three writers before 1900 and was to draw deep inspiration from each one at later stages in his own career. A critical survey of their works falls outside the scope of this Introduction, although brief details about them are in the Index of Important People.

During his years at Gaienhofen when the memory of the Franco-Prussian war was still green and the First World War not far off, it is not difficult to see why Burckhardt, a major historian who claimed, among other things, that culture is but one of history's many manifestations and that life implies a recognition of both the physical and the spiritual in human affairs, should have exerted such a profound influence on Hesse. The hopes of a new social order, based on plain human values such as tolerance and respect, that began to bloom in the aftermath of the First World War were to find enthusiastic support in Hesse. His several articles in German newspapers and magazines attest to this – in particular his letters to German youth – but worse was to come for, less than a generation later, all notion of cultural rebirth was ousted by the dream of The Third Reich. Hitler's vision of a new world-order was anathema to the one envisaged by Hesse. Yet, despite the trauma of the First World War and what he deemed the absurd rise and apparent success of Hitler, Hesse's early dreams of a new age for humanity based on spiritual values never left him.

BERN (1912–1919)

Mention has already been made of the travels undertaken by a restless and despondent husband in a marriage that was in decline. Spring walking tours through Northern Italy, summer mountain-climbing excursions and winter ski holidays in Switzerland, lecture tours in Germany and regular business trips to Munich took Hesse away from an increasingly estranged Maria. Hence his trip to the Orient in late 1911 was no real surprise; accompanied by the painter Hans Sturzenegger, he went to Ceylon, Sumatra and Malaya, was appalled by the poverty and filth and returned prematurely to Europe suffering from dysentery. His trip had been a dismal failure and it was not until he began to write *Siddhartha* that he re-encountered the wisdom of India. On his return, he and Maria decided to move to Bern. It was deemed, even if not said openly, that a change of scene might save their marriage. Besides, their eldest son's school needs now had to be considered, Maria was homesick and both she and Hermann realized that their time in Gaienhofen had reached its natural end.

At the outbreak of the First World War, their third son Martin was seriously ill with diphtheria, and there were signs of 'abnormality' in Maria's behaviour. Hesse applied for military service but was turned down because of his age, family and poor eyesight – he had volunteered despite his abhorrence of violence – only to be maligned by an irresponsible reporter as a draft evader and renegade. Hesse had good reason to feel victimised in 1914. Although he defended himself in newspaper articles, he could do nothing to change public opinion against him and so, more or less overnight, he became the object of rank invective, a national *persona non grata*.

Yet Hesse was anything but a degenerate or traitor. He went to the German embassy in Bern to offer his services and was assigned to a department that took care of German POWs. He began to run a book-distribution service for German soldiers imprisoned in Allied countries which was very successful. From January 1916 to November 1918 alone, half a million volumes were sent to internment camps in France, Hesse's main area of responsibility.

His father died in 1916, and with the groundswell of

SIDDHARTHA

public antipathy towards him mounting, Hesse sought refuge in seclusion and in silence. He turned to psycho-analysis, to the work of Freud and Jung and to therapy with Josef Lang. With Lang's help, he was able to begin what he described as the 'Weg nach Innen' (the path within), a path that he hoped would lead to self-knowl-edge and fulfilment. The profound influence of Freud, Jung, and especially Josef Lang is very visible in the fiction he wrote after 1916, as well as in the only essay that deals exclusively with the science of psychoanalysis and its relationship to literature, entitled *Künstler und Psychoanalyse* (*Artists and Psychoanalysis*), published in 1918.

It should not be forgotten, however, that Hesse, both before and after his encounter with the new world of psychology, continued to heed what he termed 'the voice of life', a throw-back perhaps to the sentiment expressed so vehemently in his letters of 1892, in which he declared that he wanted to fulfil himself as a human being. Psychoanalysis led Hesse to re-appraise himself and his situation at a time when his world had collapsed about his ears. Introspection, an important feature of his works, became relentless self-analysis which in turn led to a re-awakening and to self-transformation. It was to strengthen that 'inner voice' which Hesse had always attempted to follow. Although in public Hesse was a reject, an eccentric and outsider, he was beginning to become his own man. The first sign of this was in his total change of attitude towards the Great War.

One year before the war's end Hesse wrote a series

17

of five articles for the *Frankfurter Zeitung* in which he denounced what he saw as purposeless slaughter. His open attacks on the German state culminated in *Zarathustra's Wiederkehr* (*Zarathustra's Return*), published in January 1919, possibly Hesse's most impassioned and direct appeal to German youth. The debt to Nietzsche is seen not only in the title, but also in its fiery substance. All young people were urged to drop all identification with the 'Vaterland', with its lust for power and glory and with its promotion of political causes. He called on them to accept their individual lives, to be themselves and to live out their own destiny, for each person, Hesse argued, was his own fate.

Echoing Nietzsche, he went on to say that each had to learn to suffer and thereby to live, for to live was to suffer. The classical concept of *amor fati* does not sit very well with Hesse's belief in self-determination, although there is no denying that he knew suffering; he suffered because of this very belief. Even as a child Hesse suffered because he followed the promptings of his own heart. In suffering thus he would have found an ally in Nietzsche, for the most fundamental concern throughout Nietzsche's life was to plot the relationship between suffering and culture, or cultures. This issue was of deep concern to Hesse likewise. The views of Nietzsche serve as a crucial sub-text to these articles. *Zarathustra's Wiederkehr*, however, fell upon deaf ears, or worse, aroused acute animosity.

Incredibly, despite being physically and emotionally exhausted, his ideals undermined and his life with

Maria worsening, Hesse was able to continue his flow of short stories, literary studies, travel reports, poems, extensive entries into his diaries, and editorial work. His wartime service, psychoanalysis and watercolour painting, which he had turned to in 1916 for therapeutic reasons, helped him to retain his sanity.

When Maria was declared psychotic in October 1918 and was hospitalized, Bruno and Heiner were placed in a boarding school, and so Hesse, at long last, was 'free'. When released from his wartime job in March 1919 he immediately settled his affairs in Bern and in April left for Ticino, to the village of Montagnola, to begin his life afresh. With this move his marriage, in effect, ended. Although Maria had left hospital in March 1919 she returned there again that same summer. The following January the two sons were placed with foster-parents in the Black Forest. Hesse had learnt, not without pain, that he could not be a creative writer and simultaneously live as an ordinary citizen.

Although this view was soon to be challenged by his second wife Ruth Wenger and, after her, by Ninon Dolbin, a divorcee some eighteen years his junior, when Hesse left Bern he was resolved more than ever before to be his own man, on his own.

MONTAGNOLA (1919–1922)

Although the next stage in Hesse's life spans the years from 1919 to 1931, this section will only go as far as 1922, the year in which *Siddhartha* was published.

Readers desirous of knowing more in detail of Hesse's life – after all, he was to live another forty years – should refer to the Bibliography.

Hesse continued to follow the 'path within' for he had become convinced that there was no other way to his salvation. And it is this firm conviction, presented so often as a tenacious self-quest, that is mirrored especially well in his more popular novels and essays. According to Mileck, the years in Ticino remained ' . . . the most vibrant and productive period of his life . . .' Until 1923 Hesse rarely emerged from his hermitical retreat, although he was eager to strike up new friendships with local, like-minded people. Hence his liaison with the Swiss writer Lisa Wenger, whose daughter Ruth he was to marry in January 1924, some five months after terminating his marriage to Maria. Ruth was less than half his age, and her life had been troubled by frail health and emotional instability. Marriage only made matters worse, for both of them. Life with Hesse quickly became a physical and emotional torment for her. Their paths parted after only eleven weeks of marriage. On the verge of a nervous breakdown and also suffering from what proved to be tuberculosis of the lungs, she went to a sanatorium where she suffered repeated relapses. They were divorced in 1927.

The failure of his second marriage brought Hesse to another crisis point which led to *Steppenwolf* (1927), arguably the most autobiographical of Hesse's novels. Although analysis of this crucial novel lies outside the scope of this Introduction, the writing of *Steppenwolf* probably prevented Hesse from suicide. In a letter to Georg Reinhart dated 18 August, 1925, he doubted whether *Steppenwolf* would ever be written. Life, he laments, had become too much of a burden. For this reason, he accompanied his letter with a copy of his autobiography, *Life in Brief*, first published in 1924. Both of these texts, together with *Siddhartha*, may best be judged in the light of an earlier letter of Hesse's written in 1923, in which he clearly admitted that the root cause of his problems in life stemmed from the fact that, in his youth, the whole of his education had revolved around what he terms 'the spiritual–poetical', and that, as time went on, he had to recognize that he had become 'a hopeless Outsider'.

The reception of *Steppenwolf* was as unfavourable as that of *Siddhartha*. Yet, like its predecessor, it came to be a bestseller and, for those who wish to trace the 'development' of Hesse as a writer of prose, it is essential reading.

With the ending of the war, Hesse began a new publishing venture, *Vivos Voco*, a monthly periodical aimed at young people in particular and focusing on a new Germany, and a new social order. He was convinced that a disenchanted post-war Germany would be ripe for 'changes for the better'. However, the resurgent nationalism quickly dispelled all hopes of a new beginning and in 1921, Hesse abandoned the periodical. His career as an editor of newspapers and periodicals had come to an end. This was his last organized effort to reform society. Distressed that he continued to receive hate letters merely because he championed pacificsm and internationalism, he applied for Swiss citizenship three years later which was granted in 1924.

Hesse's reasons for leaving Germany were obvious. His new socio-political ideas together with his vision of the imminent cultural decline of Europe, and of Germany in particular, made him an unwanted rebel in his own country. His views found little sympathy among the intelligentsia. Two novels, *Demian* (1917) and *Klingsor's Letzter Sommer* (1919), and a volume of essays published in 1920 entitled *Blick ins Chaos* (*A Glance into Chaos*) gave ample evidence of his belief in the cultural decline of Western Europe which he claimed would be followed by a new cultural cycle. His intense reading of Russian writers during the First World War, especially of Tolstoy and Dostoevsky, only served to confirm him in this view. Despite his optimistic belief in a new birth or perhaps a new Renaissance, Hesse's critics denounced him for being 'defeatist' or 'alarmist' and even where his detractors accepted that cultural rebirth was a possibility, they insisted it was not to be found in Hesse's Asiatic ideal but in a return to German Idealism.

The publication in 1922 of *Siddhartha* gave his many critics yet another opportunity to slander him. Reviews of the novel in German newspapers were scathing and deeply distressing for Hesse. He was accused, among other things, of turning his back on the plight and sufferings of his own people. For modern readers, such attacks against the novel may come as a surprise but, in the Germany of the early 1920s, they were both real and persistent. Indeed, the 1920s were depressing years for Hesse. Germany had proved to be a vast disappointment. In his view, she had learnt nothing from the wars of 1870 and 1914–18. Politically and morally the country was in chaos. Clearly, the gulf between Hesse and Germany was unbridgeable long before the Nazis came to power. He must have felt relieved when his application for exile in Switzerland was approved. Exile brought Hesse little respite from work, but there is no doubt that his first twelve years there represent the golden age of his literary works.

SIDDHARTHA:
BACKGROUND

Since publication *Siddhartha* has sold over two million copies in Germany, over five million in the USA, and further millions in Japan and elsewhere. Undoubtedly one of the most influential works of German (and European) literature in the twentieth century, the novel continues to have wide appeal. The question naturally arises, what is the cause of its success and how different is it from other works of Hesse's?

In an important letter dated 26 June 1923, Hesse acknowledged that his 'sickness with life' (*Lebenskrankheit*) arose from a total preoccupation with the 'spiritual–poetical'; it was this that had led to his being what he termed 'a hopeless outsider'. This admission, coming very shortly after the publication in 1922 of what he sub-titles his 'Indic Poem', sheds invaluable light on the contents and style not only of *Siddhartha* but also of all his creative works to that date – and these include tales, legends, recollections, Italianate short stories, poems, and even romantic verse playlets.

Exclusive focus on the 'spiritual–poetical' accounts for the similarity of themes in his writings and also helps to explain their overwhelmingly confessional tone. From his earliest novels, *Peter Camenzind* (1903), *Unter Dem Rad* (*Beneath the Wheel*, 1904), *Gertrud* (1910), *Rosshalde* (1914), and the prize-winning and popular *Demian* (1919), Hesse depicts individuals trying to come to terms with their destiny.

In reply to the question 'Where do you come from?', one of Saint-Exupéry's characters replies, 'I have come from my childhood.' Hesse might have said the same. Experiences at school and attitudes at home – the sources of much of his misery – helped him, albeit painfully, to become the person he was. It is no surprise, therefore, that in his novels he reappraises his formative years which had shaped his life and thought.

Siddhartha's malaise, in part at least, stems from his 'education'. The breach between what he has been taught and what he believes he needs to experience lies at the root of his discontent. This accounts for his flight from the route planned for him by his parents, in much the same way that young Hesse fled from school in Maulbronn.

In the Eastern philosophy expounded in the *Upani-*

shads and in the *Bhagavad Gita*, the Indian texts Hesse studied most closely, he discovered a system of thought in which the serious seeker of truth is able to rise above the tyranny of the senses and ascend to that all-embracing unity which mystics sing about. In such texts, the conflict of duality is described as that between the 'higher' and 'lower' selves. The senses, according to the *Upanishads*, naturally turn outwards to the transient world of pleasure and pain (*sansara* in the novel), whereas the mind can turn 'inwards' and discover a realm described as unchanging and therefore 'real' and blissful. In these writings, Hesse found both the theoretical and practical basis for his novel. He then fleshed out the detail from his personal experiences. In this way the novel plots Siddhartha's, that is, Hesse's, progress towards an all-transcendent realm where duality no longer prevails.

To accentuate the theme of duality, Hesse has recourse to the use of a double (*Doppelgänger*), in the role of the two friends; Siddhartha's friendships with Govinda and later with Vasudeva illustrate this theme. The protagonist almost always represents the character that Hesse thought of as himself and the close friend represents what Hesse would have liked to be, or had to become, in order to fulfil himself. Seen in this light, the relationships Siddhartha develops with Govinda, the Samanas, Buddha, Kamala, Kamaswami, his own son and with Vasudeva open up interesting perspectives on the novel.

The overriding focus of the novel is on the inner

or spiritual development of the characters; Hesse is concerned with what goes on inside the soul of individuals where, in his view, the 'real' action in a human life occurs. The 'outside' world serves as no more than a convenient backdrop and the action almost always relates to the 'journey within'.

Whereas *Demian* was written in two months, *Siddhartha* took from December 1919 to May 1921 to complete. Part One – chapters one to four – was written in 1920 and appeared in the *Neuen Rundschau* newspaper. Hesse found no difficulty in completing the first four chapters, which describe how Siddhartha excels in the practices and rituals expected of a future priest, the profession that his parents want him to follow.

After such a positive start to the novel, the delay in its completion, according to Hesse, stemmed from the fact that he himself had not experienced that transcendental state of unity to which Siddhartha aspires. In order to do so, Hesse lived as a virtual semi-recluse and became totally immersed in the sacred teachings of both Hindu and Buddhist scriptures. His intention was to attain that 'completeness', which, in the novel, is the Buddha's badge of distinction. The fruits of Hesse's readings and austerities are also found in the second half of Part Two, beginning with 'The Ferryman'. The influence of the *Upanishads* lies at the heart of the mystical visions experienced by both Siddhartha and Govinda.

In turning to the Orient for inspiration Hesse was not

alone; its influence is clearly discernible in the works of Franz Werfel, Gustav Holst and in the religious organ music of Olivier Messiaen. Even before the war both Freud and Edmund Husserl had studied Eastern writings in an attempt to re-define the concept of the ego and with it a better understanding of the pysche. Spengler's *The Decline of the West* (1918–22) was an extremely influential work which paved the way for intellectuals, writers and philosophers to seek in Oriental mysticism the birth of a new cultural era.

In looking eastwards for a possible solution to the traumas of a post-First World War society, Hesse was in fact turning 'homewards'. After all, he grew up surrounded with memories of India, her gods, customs and traditions. Nor had he forgotten his own 'journey to the east' in 1911, and so it is no surprise that he should seek in Asia a spiritual answer to the crises that faced both conqueror and conquered in 1918 Europe. We know from his essay, *Eine Bibliothek der Weltliteratur* (*A Library of World Literature*), written in 1929, how well versed he was in Oriental literature: in his library, the so-called Chinese corner held more than eighty titles. The Indian spiritual works mentioned above and the writings of Schopenhauer and Nietzsche are primary sources without which *Siddhartha* would never have been written.

Hesse's efforts to reconcile opposing forces give his novels their unity and their sense of lived reality. As a result, what commentators often describe as the *coincidentia oppositorum*, the joining of opposites, is a concept that proves useful when attempting to interpret Hesse's works, especially *Siddhartha*. The peace that is known when opposites are transcended is an ideal to which spiritual seekers aspire. Hesse also aspired to it, but for most of his life it remained an ideal, seldom a reality.

Within three years of its publication *Siddhartha* was in its twenty-third edition, a remarkable achievement in face of the scathing criticism that had greeted its publication.

SIDDHARTHA:
PART ONE

The double self-projection that is so typical of Hesse's novels is seen in the friendship between Siddhartha and his companion Govinda, who is described in chapter one as Siddhartha's shadow. Although the sight of the 'prince among Brahmins' brings joy to all who see him, especially to the hearts of the young Brahmins' daughters, Siddhartha himself is not happy; he knows he lacks something. True, he has knowledge of the Atman, the Supreme Spirit that lives in the hearts of all, but he has not yet experienced what he has been told is the highest knowledge, and without such experience he will be no different from any other seeker whose understanding of God emanates solely from intense study of the scriptures.

As a consequence, he has begun to feel the seeds of discontent. Life is beginning to show him its pain and frustrations. Above all, he lacks peace of mind and so is gently brought to what German critics term a *Grenzsituation*, a crisis point, as a result of which he feels compelled to forsake home and family and join the Samanas, wandering ascetics, renowned for their unpitying self-denial. His decision sets in motion a cycle of adventures.

When he decides to leave – the novel consists of a series of departures – he is accompanied by Govinda, and both become ascetics. Their goal is to conquer themselves and thus attain transcendental bliss which, according to their holy texts, is the sole point of human existence. And so they leave, fired with the enthusiasm of youth, to face the challenges of the spiritual path. Like the colourful characters in Spanish picaresque novels of the sixteenth century who leave all behind to try their fortune on the road of life, both Brahmin sons join the Samanas with an air of great expectation.

Three years with the ascetics are sufficient for Siddhartha to realize that the very knowledge acquired from their austerities is a major barrier to self-realization, the ultimate reality. Further progress must come from elsewhere. The 'bliss inexpressible through words', a verse from one of the *Upanishads* quoted by Govinda when Siddhartha questions the value of their pursuit, still remains a dream. The rest of the novel traces Siddhartha's journey towards that state of inexpressible bliss. From the outset of his quest Siddhartha knows that, on the spiritual path, no effort is ever wasted.

With the arrival of the Buddha, the search for self-realization seems over, but not for Siddhartha who, after his austerities at home and with the Samanas, has learnt that systems of belief and doctrines imposed by others may indeed show a way, but do not necessarily lead to the goal. Their path was not the path prompted by his inner voice.

The eagerly awaited meeting with The Illustrious One occurs in chapter three and results in another departure; Govinda joins the Buddha and both leave the 'prince of Brahmins' to seek his path, alone. To all who meet him there is no doubt that the Buddha is 'complete', that he has attained what all seekers desire, 'enlightenment', that, indeed, he is a God amongst men. His enigmatic smile is an outward expression of a soul at one with everything, for it is at peace with itself. This is the state of being Siddhartha seeks, the absence of which is the cause of his present sorrow and wanderings.

Although the purpose of the Buddha's teaching is salvation from suffering, Siddhartha is convinced that neither the sage nor his doctrines are able to convey the secret of the experience of enlightenment and, for Siddhartha, no other experience is acceptable. The Buddha leaves Siddhartha as lovingly as he had met him. This contrasts with the reaction of the leader of the Samanas when he learns of Siddhartha's intention to leave the Order. It also contrasts with the despondent goodbyes of Siddhartha's parents, and with the rather fretful farewells between Govinda and Siddhartha.

After twenty years of togetherness they decide on separate paths. With the 'loss' of Govinda, Siddhartha's 'servant, lance-bearer and shadow', the ascetic side of his nature is cast off to make way for his sensuous involvement with Kamala. He will seek in her what he failed to find as an ascetic.

Chapter four in Part One describes Siddhartha as 'awakened', a term usually associated with the Buddha (the Awakened One). But it is appropriate here, for when he is stripped of everything, family, friends, doctrines, rituals, and the support of his fellow-monks, he is able to draw closer to what may be termed his 'real self'. This is why now he sees the creation anew and why objects in it have a reality and a meaning which, if properly understood, say something valid about its Maker.

After years of asceticism, it is no surprise that a reaction should have come about and that the newly-awakened seeker should find a fresh delight in the world and believe, rightly or wrongly, that he has been reborn. The world, however, has not altered one iota; what has changed is Siddhartha's viewpoint and therefore his attitude towards himself, towards others and the circumambient universe, a volte-face that is a necessary step, so it would seem, in the search for true understanding and happiness. The change is 'within', because Hesse was convinced that any change worthy of the name could not come from anywhere else. In 1919 he had already claimed: 'What we can and should change is ourselves: our impatience, our egoism (spiritual egoism too), our sense of hurt, our lack of love and forbearance. Any other change in the world, even when done for the best intentions, I consider as useless.'

Hesse's belief in the primacy of inner change accords with the spirit of the teachings, by no means exclusively Eastern, found in the *Upanishads* and *Bhagavad Gita*.

What should not be underestimated is Siddhartha's decision not to follow the Buddha's Way. How many sincere seekers would have the courage not to follow an accepted master? Does this conscious rejection make Siddhartha the type of hero Nietzsche would praise as *Übermensch*? For now Siddhartha is isolated, cut off from community life, in much the same way that Haller in *Steppenwolf* is cut off from the life of the herd.

In Vedantic tradition, it was – and still is – not at all uncommon for young adults in India to leave home and family in the search for an accepted master or teacher, called a guru. Although there have been many gurus, there was only one Buddha and to reject him must be viewed as unconventional. This deviation from convention is characteristic of Hesse, himself highly unconventional. Siddhartha's action has found ever-growing support, especially today when many more people want to follow their own path. For those who think that Siddhartha exemplifies the model student of ancient Vedantic teachings, however, the lives of modern Indian saints – Nityananda and Muktananda – offer valuable, contrastive reading.

Three factors contributed to Hesse's preparation of

the text of Siddhartha. Firstly, his rediscovery of India's sacred writings, secondly his psychoanalytical sessions with Jung, and thirdly his deep and repeated reading of *Tao Te Ching*, of Lao-tsu.

Although relatively brief, Part One introduces us to familiar themes in Hesse's work; the conflict between discipline and the heart, the desire to 'go it alone', the role of the two friends, the courage to listen to one's inner voice, the search for spiritual knowledge, etc. What is different is the setting and the choice of the sixth century (556–476 BC), the dates of the historical Buddha. This aside, the subject matter is well in keeping with Hesse's fictional output.

Mention has been made of his trip to the Orient in 1911 and this gave rise to a spate of works, the first of which was published in 1913 under the title *Aus Indien* (*From India*). Eastern influences – in particular Chinese – are seen in a number of stories and fairy tales (not mentioned among the novels preceding *Siddhartha*) such as *Robert Aghion* (1912), in 1913 *Der Dichter* (*The Poet*), in 1914 *Das Haus der Träume* (*The House of Dreams*), in 1915, *Faldum*, in 1916 *Der schwere Weg* (*The Trying Road*) and in 1918 *Iris*. All these may be considered as preludes to *Siddhartha*. Considering Hesse's family background it is not surprising that he looked beyond Europe – to the extreme annoyance of his fellow-countrymen – and focused on Eastern sacred writings to make sense of the senselessness of four years of war. He had re-read the works of Schopenhauer and had felt compelled to re-examine his own beliefs, attuitudes and life-style. The years that preceded the outbreak of the Great War were extremely busy ones for Hesse but it is clear that the seeds of *Siddhartha* had been sown long before the novel saw the light of day. A study of the writings of Hesse up until 1922 proves that *Siddhartha* was neither out of keeping with Hesse's literary repertoire nor a callous attempt, as his detractors claimed, to dismiss the plight of Germans in the aftermath of the First World War.

In a letter dated 1931, he is at pains to show that in the novel he attempted to set down the foundations of a faith that would help young people to begin their lives again. Hesse went on to claim quite seriously that his novel was 'an attempt to formulate that which was most important', and that the reader should make a thorough study of its every word, in much the same way that theological students study the Bible. Hence, far from turning his back on his fellow-countrymen, especially on German youth, he was attempting to create, through his writing, a better world and future for them.

Bearing in mind the solemn intentions of its author when he wrote the text, Part Two, which comprises eight chapters, reveals what, in his view, was the most important thing in life.

SIDDHARTHA:
PART TWO (CHAPTERS 5–8)

Siddhartha's refusal to follow the Buddha is in keeping with Nietzsche's statement in *Also sprach Zarathustra* (*Thus Spake Zarathustra*) that '. . . one repays a teacher badly if one always wants to remain nothing but a pupil'. Not that Siddhartha had ever been a devotee of Buddha, but he had been and still was a seeker. It is clear that Hesse is urging Siddhartha to seek his true self and to do so without props. What the Self meant for Hesse will be clarified later but, from the outset, Siddhartha's quest may be seen as a natural outcome of tendencies, influences and events peculiar to Hesse's own life.

In chapter five, Siddhartha seeks his place 'in this world'. He becomes attracted to what hitherto he had termed Maya – the veil of illusion – and is content to explore its 'reality', something he had always dismissed. He infers that Buddha attained self-realization by seeking it in his own way and listening to his inner voice. Siddhartha is prepared to ignore Buddha's precepts but not his example. This is not conventional Vedantic teaching, as Siddhartha, as an ex-Brahmin and ex-Samana monk, would know instinctively.

When the ferryman takes him across the river, the world of the senses becomes Siddhartha's new playground. Hence his involvement with the stunningly beautiful and rich courtesan Kamala. But in order to 'enjoy' her company he has to become truly worldly, and thus finds employment with Kamaswami, the rich merchant. The extent of his worldliness is recorded in the poem he offers Kamala in return for a kiss. Often overlooked by commentators, this poem reveals the new Siddhartha, as a man of the world, intent on adapting as quickly as possible to its ways:

> '... Better, thought the young Samana,
> To make sacrifices to the fair Kamala
> Than to offer sacrifices to the gods.'

Such blasphemy shows how completely he has broken away from his former self. In his efforts to taste the world, Siddhartha is as zealous as he was when serving the spirit. Here is the duality, present in Hesse's major novels, depicted in Nietzsche's works as the conflict between Apollo and Dionysus, and one that Siddhartha desperately seeks to transcend. If Govinda represents the rule of discipline, it is clear that, without him, Siddhartha is free to plunge into the world of sensual enjoyment. No man can serve two masters – God and Mammon – at one and the same time. He has served the spirit without reaching his goal; now he will serve his senses.

He views Kamala's conditions of acceptance – fine clothes, fine shoes, and money for presents – as trifles and is thus eager to begin. One deep kiss from Kamala suffices to launch him on the path of worldly wisdom. Armed with what in worldly terms are absurd qualifications – he can think, wait and fast! – he begins his

new life. Whether this recourse to intense sensual grati-
fication will lead him to his final goal remains to be
seen but, at this stage, he firmly believes that what he
is doing is for the best.

Despite the inappropriateness of his skills, Siddhartha is successful at his work and is able to spend
many hours with Kamala. It is from her that his present
life gains its meaning and value, not from making
money for Kamaswami. He has an air of indifference
in all his dealings with the world of work, a detachment
which contrasts vividly with his master who is easily
upset if business is bad.

Siddhartha cannot, however, erase all trace of his
past life. It has left its mark so deeply on his soul that
he is forced to recognize that, despite all, he is still
separated from his fellow-beings. In a manner reminiscent of Buddha himself, his heart opens to the
suffering of humanity and is saddened at its lack of
discrimination. Humans cause their own anguish and,
what is worse, create it for each other as well. Aware
of the gulf between himself and the common folk, he
draws closer to Kamala, who understands Siddhartha
better than Govinda did.

The notion of the 'outsider' surfaces again at the
start of chapter seven in which the highly prosperous
Siddhartha begins to feel the discontent which, years
before, had driven him from the home of his pious
parents. Inertia, despondency and nausea betray a
deeper malaise; his inner voice is now silent; inwardly
he is 'dead'. To compensate, he immerses himself in

reckless gambling. Now winning is no longer a game but a compulsion and, in the addictive and futile cycle that gambling creates, he becomes old, weary and sick. His sickness is of the soul, as it was at the beginning of the novel, but he now suffers from *Weltschmerz*, weariness of living in the world.

Then, inevitably, a turning-point is reached. For the first time during their intimacy, grief and tiredness can be heard behind Kamala's words. Siddhartha realizes that twenty years of pleasure have passed by, but he is no nearer his goal. To make things worse, he notices his first grey hairs – a shock to a man famed in his youth for his vigour and beauty. On Kamala's once exquisitely chiselled face he sees signs of fading splendour, the first lines under her eyes, wrinkles near the corners of her mouth. When he leaves her, he is haunted by fear of old age and of death, a fear that haunts both Klingsor and Harry Haller.

That night he tries to sleep off his misery, a misery deepened by his awareness of his totally dissolute life. At daybreak, he has a dream, a favourite literary device of Hesse's used long before his sessions with Jung and his readings of Freud for whom, as we know, dreams were the *via regia* to the unconscious. In his dream he learns that he has thrown away all that was good and of value in himself. He is in the grip of another *Grenzsituation*, which compels him to re-examine his former life.

Dreams in Hesse's novels are clues to the state of a character's soul. The death of the songbird in Kamala's golden cage, which is the crux of his dream, reminds Siddhartha of his former ways. It is the memory of his previous disciplined life that makes him leave his love, home and secure job in the world. When Kamala releases her rare songbird, the symbolism is clear; her past life has also finished for ever. Now pregnant with Siddhartha's child, eleven years will pass before they meet again. Although neither can foresee the circumstances of their next meeting, both will learn invaluable soul-lessons from it, especially Siddhartha, who is gradually learning to accept all that life throws at him.

Once he has left, he falls prey to despair and thoughts of suicide. Like the young Hesse when at school in Bad Boll and Hans Giebenrath in the novel *Beneath the Wheel*, Siddhartha's inner tensions have reached breaking point, like a bird hatching. This is the central image in the novel *Demian*, and very pertinent here: 'The egg is the world. Whoever wants to be born must first destroy a world. The bird is flying to God. The name of the God is Abraxas.'

At the river's edge, Siddhartha is faced with a decision. He has destroyed the old world, will he now fly to God or enter oblivion? Then, redemptively, the mystical sound of Om arises within him and his moment of crisis passes. Abraxas, the Gnostic power or spirit which reconciles the godly and the satanic comes in the guise of Om, the supreme symbol for the unity of God, the world and the individual soul. Siddhartha is saved and then enters a deep sleep from which he arises spiritually rejuvenated.

The man who awakens to find Govinda standing over him is a new man, so new in fact that he is unrecognized. The change that has taken place in Siddhartha is like a resurrection. The Lord Krishna tells Arjuna in the *Bhagavad Gita* that, 'On this path endeavour is never wasted, nor can it ever be repressed. Even a very little of its practice protects one from great danger.' In Siddhartha's hour of greatest need, the memory of his former practices arises in his tormented soul to remind him of his true stature. Inwardly he is, and has remained, a 'prince among Brahmins'. Govinda, however, continues to 'live according to the rule, preach the gospel, collect alms and then move on. It is always the same . . .' Though Siddhartha experiences more than Govinda, this is important only if it brings about a greater inner change.

The real point of Siddhartha's transformation – and this largely explains his present euphoric happiness – is that he is a child once again, that he can hear the bird in his breast, that he can re-love himself. Moreover, he is quietly convinced that his decision to leave home, Govinda and Buddha has been justified and that the root cause of his discontent can be put down to one thing: over-exertion. He has spent too long trying to 'become' what he wanted to be rather than 'being' what he is. The crucial distinction in German philosophical thought between *sein* (to be) and *werden* (to become), so well formulated by Goethe and so clearly expounded in the *Upanishads* centuries before him, has now been understood by the world-weary Siddhartha. It is a distinction that will be reinforced in the following chapter when Siddhartha decides to join Vasudeva and begins to listen to the river. All further events in the novel should be seen in the light of what he discovers from the river, just as all past events in his life can be most usefully interpreted in the light of the ontological difference between being and becoming.

Chapter eight, the second third of the novel, now draws to a close. Those who see a tripartite structure to the text – and the reasons for so doing are numerous – point to the symbol of the river to argue their case. Siddhartha grew up on the banks of one side of the river, crossed over to the 'other' side to experience the 'world', and returns to the river in order to stay with it. Each stage lasts approximately twenty years and may be seen to represent the three constituents of man: the mind, body and soul. The first four chapters reveal the ascetic ideals of Siddhartha in which he is filled with the traditional teachings of his caste. This is followed by his rejection of all practices and disciplines imposed 'from without' and by his surrender to the glamour of the world based on a *carpe diem* attitude towards life. This in turn leads to self-revulsion and to the third and final stage in his evolution, as a seeker on a lonely and arduous spiritual way. If transcendence is his goal, it will be in this closing section that he will secure it.

In terms of ancient Indian philosophy, the three stages above also relate to three of the stages that span human existence: 'brahmacarin', 'grihastha' and

'vanaprastha'. The first relates to the state of an unmar-
ried religious student; the second to the duties of a
house-holder (having a family and a job, etc.), the third
to withdrawal to the forest and living the life of an
anchorite. There is a fourth phase, relevant to Siddhartha, and that is called 'sanyasin', one who has
'renounced' worldly affairs to reflect on ultimate truths.
In terms of structure, it is possible to relate the above
stages to the story of Siddhartha.

One interesting aspect of the novel's two-part structure is its relationship to the Buddha's four noble truths
(Part One) and to his eight-fold path (Part Two), which
together form twelve chapters, the number in the novel.
In support of this view, there are several features
common to both: they share the same name
(Siddhartha), they break away from family tradition,
they 'go their own way', seek liberation, leave behind
'family and child', leave other ascetics and their doctrines and discover that self-realization lies within their
own self. Moreover, and this is not commonly known,
Hesse wrote another chapter called 'Devadetta' which
seems to be a corruption of 'Devadatta', a very common
Sanskrit name meaning 'God-given', which, had he
included, would have brought the total to thirteen chapters, thus breaking the numerical corespondence with
the Buddha's teachings.

As chapter eight closes the symbol of the river pre-
dominates, closely associated with the syllable Om, the
sound that saves Siddhartha from destruction. He
learns that the river, although ever-changing and ever-

flowing, always remains the same, is always 'present'. The river simply is; it is not a 'has been' or a 'will be'. It is everywhere itself, simultaneously. Siddhartha realizes that his life too is a river and that all life flows into it. All that exists is in its waters; past and future dissolve in the all-encompassing, eternal, present moment, the sound of which is Om. Not until chapter eleven does Siddhartha experience the cosmic import of Om but, for now, he is content to remain by the river and therefore 'spiritually' ready to meet Vasudeva, the ferry-man.

SIDDHARTHA PART TWO: CHAPTERS (9–12)

The decision to stay by the river arose in Siddhartha's own heart: such decisions should always be followed and so he becomes Vasudeva's apprentice. In so doing, he rightly believes that he will learn what he needs to know to attain self-knowledge. It is the river itself, explains Vasudeva, that has drawn him and it is from the river that he will learn how to listen. And then, enigmatically, he lets slip the comment that Siddhartha '... will learn the other thing too'. What that 'other thing' is Vasudeva will not say and it is clear to his listener that whatever it is, it cannot be described in words.

Thousands have been ferried across, continues Vasudeva, but only a few have not seen the river as an obstacle. To these few alone has the river become holy.

Vasudeva's words echo those of Lord Krishna '... Among thousands of men scarcely one strives for perfection, and even amongst those who gain occult powers, perchance but one knows Me in truth.'

Is this 'the other thing' that Vasudeva has just mentioned? Certainly Siddhartha, Govinda and the Samanas have been striving for perfection but who, in truth, really knows the Supreme? The Buddha? Vasudeva? At this point in his journey, Siddhartha is convinced that he does not know, but somehow intuits that he is close. The decision to stay marks a major turning-point in the narrative and, consequently, in Siddhartha's life.

In the world of Kamala and Kamaswami, the three skills of knowing how to fast, wait and think seemed little enough. With Vasudeva, there is only one teacher and one lesson: to listen with a still heart. And, with practice, that is what Siddhartha achieves. He learns so well that he and Vasudeva become like brothers; Vasudeva fulfils the same role for Siddhartha as Siddhartha had for Govinda.

In time, Siddhartha learns from the river its most treasured secret; that time does not exist. In a beautiful passage in the *Bhagavad Gita*, a recurring sub-text in the chapters that follow, Lord Krishna tells his beloved disciple Arjuna that '... there was never a time when I was not and there will never be a time when I shall cease to be.'

By listening to the river, Siddhartha discovers the truth of Krishna's words. The unity of all life, the experience of which is the fruit of self-realization, is a law that the Buddha lived daily and one that daily contact with the river brings ever closer to Siddhartha. Listening to its eternal flow dispenses with the need for doctrines, rituals and disciplines. The two ferry-men have no cause to speak. Their hearts and souls are so finely attuned to each other that verbal communication is rendered obsolete. Both have their minds fixed on the Eternal. Years pass by and outwardly nothing seems to 'happen' in their lives; they have reached that point where outer events no longer can affect them, so indissolubly linked are they to the one presence in everything.

Critics rightly describe Hesse's novels as 'landscapes of the soul', a description that fits the stark confessional tone of this and other narratives. External events are only 'real' insofar as they impinge upon inner realities. A central teaching of Vedantic philosophy, and one already mentioned, is that we cannot change events. We can only change our reaction to events. This is a hard pill for Siddhartha to swallow, even harder for Western readers. Its truth is borne out in a series of events, however, beginning with the impending death of the Buddha.

The Buddha's devotees, which now include Kamala and her son, flock from all corners to receive his last blessings. Kamala is bitten by a deadly snake near the ferry and carried by Vasudeva to his hut, where she is immediately recognized by Siddhartha, who now sees that he has a son. More poignantly, he also sees that

Kamala is dying, and that he can do nothing to stop it. The poison, inevitably, will do its work. The irony is that Kamala had come to see Buddha's death but, instead, is compelled to face her own. Before she dies, however, she learns that Siddhartha has found peace, although unknown to her, that peace is soon to be shattered by the antics and flight of their son. In a deeply moving scene, both Kamala and Siddhartha are 'joined' again; she recognizes that he is and yet is not the same man. Outwardly, he may seem no different but, inwardly, he has been re-baptized, dipped in God!

With the passing of Kamala, Siddhartha is suddenly left to deal with a son he has never known. The ferry-hut is no refuge for a boy accustomed to 'the good life' in the city. And when, after an act of defiance reminiscent of Hesse himself when at school, the boy runs away, both men realise that it is for the best. The usually reticent Vasudeva soothingly explains that everyone born into this world has their own path to tread, a path mapped out in one's karma. In a dialogue again based on the *Gita*, Vasudeva wisely concludes: 'If you were to die ten times for him, you would not alter his destiny in the slightest'. The way to follow one's own path is through detachment, a key teaching of the *Gita* and one which Vasudeva and Buddha adhered to religiously.

Siddhartha's new-found human love for his son brings with it not joy but pain. Attempting to win his son's affection only results in greater isolation. Yet he persists, for it is the first time in his life that he has ever been able to love another so completely. Initially, fear of losing his son prevented him from heeding Vasudeva's advice. When his son finally flees, Siddhartha learns an invaluable soul-lesson. The source of their conflict ran deep and no one but Vasudeva could predict the outcome. The boy leaves and plays no more part in the novel. But that does not mean that he is forgotten. His action reminds us of the time when Siddhartha left home with Govinda to join the Samanas. The pain and anguish suffered then by Siddhartha's parents are what Siddhartha now experiences. He is made to endure what he once caused his own parents to suffer.

Although Siddhartha attempts to follow his son, he knows his mission is futile. Standing at the entrance to what had once been Kamala's beautiful pleasure garden, his past rises before him, in much the same way that it did when he was tempted to suicide by the river. Grief-stricken, he leaves and sits down in the dusty road and repeats Om, the indestructible sound that is the name and symbol of Brahman. Through the loss of his son, Siddhartha learns the rare virtue of detachment, a necessary step on the way to wisdom.

Hours later, his guru Vasudeva appears. This is no surprise for a true sage acts and speaks only when necessary. Not a word passes between them; sometimes much more is 'said' by being left unsaid.

The change in Siddhartha that Kamala noticed continues and although he does not share the thoughts and views of ordinary people, he shares with them life's urges and desires. The pain suffered at the loss of his son still irks him and, in a rather strange way, draws him closer to the man-in-the-street. For what separates the sage from the rest, we are told, is that the sage is conscious of the unity of all life. Paradoxically, this sense of unity both differentiates Siddhartha from others and draws him closer to them. Knowledge of this unity is the source of the calm contentment seen in Vasudeva's old face. He knows its truth and sees it as his task to help Siddhartha to know it in experience.

In chapter eleven Siddhartha learns the final lesson. He listens more attentively to the river and thus is able to re-connect with the past that lives on inside him. Hence the play of memory that dominates these 'reflections' in the river's water. Invariably, he sees his past rise before him. Reminded of his father, he wonders whether life's events repeat in a fateful circle. Still smarting from the wound of his son's flight, he decides to lay bare his heart to Vasudeva who, once again, brings him to the river's edge. He listens and becomes aware of the unity of sound like a cosmic dance. Over and above all else, he hears the healing sound of Om, the same sound that has saved him twice from self-destruction. Ultimately, Siddhartha learns what Vasudeva has known and lived all along. By surrendering to the unity everywhere, inner peace may be attained. It is the river's greatest lesson and one now understood, no matter how fleetingly, by Siddhartha, who witnesses yet another of life's farewells.

How should Vasudeva's silent retreat into the 'forest',

'into the unity of all things' be interpreted? If we agree that he has nothing more to accomplish, then the following verses from chapter three of the *Gita* may help us to understand his action:

' . . . the soul who meditates on the Self, is content to serve the Self, and rests satisfied within the Self; there remains nothing more for him to accomplish. He has nothing to gain by the performance or non-performance of action. His welfare depends not on any contribution that an earthly creature can make.'

It is clear from the comparison between Govinda and Siddhartha that, although systems have their place in the scheme of things, those who in the novel have attained self-realization, Buddha, Vasudeva and Siddhartha, all follow their own path, a path that may find its source in the Sanskrit term 'swa-tantra', which translates loosely as 'that which has the system within itself'. Listening to one's inner voice, a constant in Hesse's works, seems to be the key to unlocking the system within. This is what Siddhartha does, and no doubt it is what, one day, Govinda will also do.

Govinda is to learn a great deal from his meeting with Siddhartha, not least of which is the claim that wisdom is not at all communicable. 'Knowledge', claims Siddhartha, 'can be communicated, but not wisdom'. He goes on to explain that the half-truths which most of us live by arise from trying to put into words the ineffable core of spiritual truth. Just as we can tell a tree by its fruits, so are there sure signs of a soul that has attained union. In the novel, the silence, compassion and beatific smile of Vasudeva are those signs. He acts and speaks only when necessary, the hallmark of true spiritual wisdom.

More significant is Siddhartha's claim that wisdom cannot be taught. The duality that spiritual teachers refer to is a necessary teaching tool but is not the whole picture. What then is the whole picture? In the novel, it takes the form of a mystical vision. Siddhartha's visions are mystical in the sense that they reveal 'consciousness of the identity of one's own inner being with that of all things' which, according to Schopenhauer, 'is a state which mystics achieve in subjective experience'. But since this experience cannot be communicated, it reaches the limits of philosophy, of language and, most crucially for spiritual aspirants, the end of their striving. What else explains the 'beatific smile' of Buddha, Vasudeva and lastly of Siddhartha himself? Is it not the outward sign of self-fulfilment in which all dualism has been transcended? The theme of dualism had of course a very significant role in Hesse's life and, as a consequence, in this and all his major works.

True to his experience, and in accord with Indian philosophical concepts of Advaita (non-duality), which is the essential teaching in the *Bhagavad Gita* and in the books of the *Upanishads*, Siddhartha points to the unity that can only be truly known in experience, and which, necessarily, transcends all notions – for him utterly false notions – of duality. After all, what do good and bad, high and low relate to, if not to a third point that contains both? In his discourse on the stone, we come to the philosophical core of Siddhartha's 'message', and of the novel. In a beautiful passage Siddhartha states:

'This stone is stone: it is also animal, God, and Buddha. I do not respect and love it because it was one thing and will become something else, but because it has already long been everything and always is everything. I love it just because it is a stone, because today and now it appears to me a stone . . . There are stones that feel like oil or soap, that look like leaves or sand, and each one is different and worships Om in its own way; each one is Brahman. At the same time it is very much stone, oily or soapy, and that is just what pleases me and seems wonderful and worthy of worship . . .'

In this love of and for the creation, not for its own sake, but for the sake of its Creator, it is clear that Siddhartha has come to the same level of experience as his preceptor and spiritual guide, Vasudeva. In what is termed his final doctrine he speaks of the one thing needed for mankind to live in peace and happiness: love. Love for this world, this creation, for others and for oneself. Govinda is taken aback. Although a seeker all his life, he finds such notions strange, even crazy. Unable to come to terms with what he has heard – Govinda would naturally baulk at anyone who dismisses 'teachings' as mere words – he nevertheless acknowledges Siddhartha's pure and radiant presence, a sure sign of saintliness, and thus he bows before him.

Govinda then asks Siddhartha to give him something to help him on his way. Looking into his face, Siddhartha sees suffering, continual seeking and continual failure. He simply asks Govinda to kiss his forehead, an act that enables Govinda to experience Siddhartha's description of the unity of all life. The source of what ensues – Govinda's cosmic vision – is to be found in chapter eleven of the *Bhagavad Gita*, entitled 'The Universal Form', in which the prince Arjuna asks Lord Krishna to reveal Himself in all His glory. With the aid of a 'divine' eye given to him by Krishna, Arjuna 'sees' the divine forms of the Lord.

Likewise through grace, Govinda 'sees' a timeless panorama of humanity performing a myriad of disparate but simultaneous actions in which birth and death are seen to be recurrent changes of state. There is no death in what can be best described as an eternal cycle of events. Undoubtedly, therefore, embedded in this trance or vision of Govinda's, is a trace of Nietzsche's doctrine of eternal recurrence but without his strongly individual view of what that doctrine – a source of deep dissension amongst philosophers – implies. In the context of the novel, it is the mystical experience of unity that matters, which is why the causal flow of time has ceased; all the faces seen are those of Siddhartha, whose beatific smile is exactly the same as that of the divine Buddha.

This mystical vision of timelessness, very similar to what Siddhartha himself experiences in the previous chapter, is what Govinda is given to help him on his way. It is a magnificent gesture of magnanimity and a fitting gift for an aspirant distinguished by his undaunted pertinacity. He is made to experience the truth that wisdom can neither be taught nor communicated in words and that what he has 'seen' has its source in his own being. Above all else, however, it is the feeling of love which now overwhelms him and which, shown as a smile, closes the text. Not only, therefore, does Siddhartha bestow on his former companion a vision of cosmic unity, but also the experience of universal love, the essence of his 'doctrine'. His smile, no different from that of the Illustrious One, has the power to evoke in Govinda the memory of 'everything that he had ever loved . . . of everything that had been of value and holy in his life'.

It is not commonly known that Hesse changed the ending to the novel. In the original version, Govinda returned one year later to the river to discover from a young ferryman that Siddhartha, like Vasudeva, had taken himself off to the forest. We can speculate as to why Hesse changed his mind but it would seem to have to do with personal experience. Just as he had been unable to continue with the latter half of Part Two until he had 'lived' what Siddhartha was to experience, similarly he changed the ending because he himself had not reached that point or nirvana in his own development.

Govinda also learns from his encounter – probably his last – with Siddhartha to trust in Providence and in his own efforts and, like David Copperfield, never to separate the two. He learns that he has not been left behind on the dusty road of life and that what others may have called his (and Siddhartha's) airy dreams of youth were, and are, pure inner realities that cannot be gainsaid. His zest for the spiritual life has been renewed and whatever now befalls him in the daily round will be set against his vision of unity, his vision of love. Armed with this, he will be well able to accept life's dichotomies and, in time, transcend them.

He has learnt the supreme importance of the need to love the world, humanity, oneself and the need to respond to one's inner voice. Siddhartha reached his mystical heights because he was guided by his heart and always tried to act to the heart, to the inner reality. Not content with words, he felt impelled to touch the inner, truer meaning of life. Siddhartha's experiences taught him how to reach out to the heart of a brother, of a group and, finally, to the heart of humanity itself. The lives of Siddhartha and Vasudeva show a continual aspiration to increase the consciousness of God within their own being. In concentrating upon the light within, they both come to recognize the perennial teaching that the same light shines in every living soul, even in the animal and mineral kingdoms, as it does through the etheric worlds, and this makes possible the type of cosmic vision seen by Govinda. There is no doubt also that Govinda's faith has received a boost:

faith not merely in the sense of belief, but faith as an inner quality, an inner knowing of God.

He will remember to the last Siddhartha's and the Buddha's heavenly smile, that symbol of a soul that has been liberated from 'sansara'. Instead of restless pressure and effort, the never-satisfied and never-dying hope that constitutes the life-dream of those caught up in the ways of this lower world, each of us can attain that peace that is beyond understanding, that ocean-like calmness of the spirit, whose mere reflection in the countenance is a complete and certain gospel.

Govinda learns that wisdom cannot be taught, for what seems right, of value, and wise to one man often seems nonsense to another. In a letter to a Persian reader in 1958, Hesse claimed that his novel sought to establish that which was common to all forms of worship and beliefs. In a strange way, therefore, Hesse, like his parents before him, was a missionary, advocating religious unity and brotherhood but without the need to convert. Siddhartha preaches tolerance, understanding and patience: three much needed virtues to readers in 1922 and that are still highly relevant today.

HERMANN HESSE: SELECT BIBLIOGRAPHY

Works by Hesse: in German:

In 1987 Suhrkamp published the complete works – 12 volumes – in paperback. This replaced their earlier (standard) edition, also in 12 volumes, published in 1970.

1) *Gesammelte Werke in zwolf Bänden*, Frankfurt am Main, 1987 (Suhrkamp,Taschenbuch.1600). In this edition *Siddhartha* is found in volume 5, pp. 353–471.

2) *Gesammelte Briefe. In Zsarb. mit Heiner Hesse hrsg. von Ursula und Volker Michels*.4 Bde. Frankfurt am M.: Suhrkamp, 1973–86. These are the collected letters of Hesse edited in 4 volumes by Ursula and Volker Michels in collaboration with Heiner Hesse (Hesse's second son).

Other novels of Hesse translated into English:
1) *Peter Camenzind*
2) *The Prodigy* (*Beneath the Wheel*)
3) *Demian*
4) *The Journey to the East*
5) *The Glass Bead Game*

Major studies of Hesse's life and work: (1) in English:

1) Mileck, Joseph, *Hermann Hesse: Life and Art*, University of California Press, 1978. By far the best study in English (to date) of the life, work and times of Hesse

2) Mileck, Joseph, *H. Hesse, Biography and Bibliography*, 2 vols, University of California Press, 1977

3) Freedman, Ralph, *Hermann Hesse: a pilgrim of crisis*, Jonathan Cape, London, 1979

(2) in German:

1) Unseld, Siegfried: *Hermann Hesse – Werk und Wirkungsgeschichte*, Frankfurt am M., 1986
2) Cheong, Kyung Yang: *Mystische Elemente aus West und Ost im Werk Hermann Hesses*, Frankfurt am M. / Bern, 1991
3) Schneider, Christian Immo: *Hermann Hesse*, München, 1991
4) Karalaschwili, Reso,: *Hermann Hesse. Charakter und Weltbild*, Frankfurt am M., 1993

On Siddhartha:

The most exhaustive study to date of *Siddhartha*, from conception to publication including its reception by the German public in 1922 and what it has meant for generations since is to be found, in German, in:

Michels, Volker, *Materialen zu Hermann Hesses Siddhartha*, 2 Bde, Frankfurt am M., 1975–6

Studies (in English) on the major novels, including *Siddhartha*:

1) Boulby, Mark, *Hermann Hesse. His Mind and Art*, New York, 1967
2) Mileck, Joseph: see above
3) Otten, Anna, *Hesse Companion*, Albuquerque, USA, 1977
4) Ziolkowski, Theodore, *The novels of Hermann Hesse. A study in theme and structure*, Princeton, USA, 1965

NB The periodic international Hermann Hesse

Kolloquium held in Calw, Hesse's birthplace, publishes up-to-date studies of Hesse's works. Most of the material, however, is in German.

GLOSSARY OF SANSKRIT, HINDU, BUDDHISTIC AND GERMAN TERMS MENTIONED IN SIDDHARTHA

Advaita: non-duality, identity of spirit and matter. The philosophical belief that underlies the teaching in the *Bhagavad Gita* and *Upanishads*. There is only one Consciousness, one Supreme Spirit, despite multiplicity; this is the 'ultimate truth' in the text, known to Vasudeva and Buddha.

Atman: breath, principle of life, the individual soul; in the grammar of Sanskrit it is also used as the reflexive pronoun: oneself.

Bhagavad Gita: A series of discourses between Lord Krishna and the warrior-prince Arjuna from which flow the essential teachings of Indian philosophy, equivalent to the New Testament. It forms one episode in India's Great Epic, the *Mahabharata*, written later than the 'classical' *Upanishads*.

Brahman: from root 'bhri' to grow, expand, increase. Hence the 'swelling of the soul' that leads to the meaning of the self-existent, impersonal Spirit, the Absolute, the Eternal, the universal essence from which all created things emanate or with which they are identified and to which they return ; not generally an object of worship, but rather of meditation and knowledge.

Brahmin: not to be confused with **Brahman!** The priestly class, highest of the four divisions in ancient Hindu society; strictly speaking, one who knows and repeats the Vedas, e.g. Siddhartha.

Buddha: from the Sanskrit root 'budh' 'to wake up', hence, The Awakened or Enlightened One. Hence Buddha is not a proper name but a title.

Chandogya Upanishad: See under **Upanishads.**

Doppelgänger: literally 'double', a common device in modern novels in which the author and the main character are generally one and the same person; a favourite device of Hesse's.

Cycle of rebirth: reincarnation is an essential belief in the East, not only in India. When we become one with our Creator (the heaven of Christianity) the chains of rebirth are broken for ever. For many, such a state (bliss) is the sole goal of human existence.

Gotama: Buddha's family name in the last of his earthly incarnations in the sixth century BC.

Govinda: literally 'cowman'; one who looks after the cows; Govinda is one of the thousand names of Krishna; another Govinda was the teacher of Shankara, founder of the monastic order in India; his commentaries on the *Gita* and *Upanishads* are accepted masterpieces.

Grenzsituation: literally a 'borderline situation', a crisis point, which necessitates immediate action.

Guru: a Sanskrit term having multiple meanings, the basic one being 'heavy or weighty', also meant a spiritual parent or preceptor from whom a youth receives the initiatory mantra or prayer and instruction in the 'sastras' (rules, sacred teachings). Hence the modern usage.

Karma: literally 'action, works'. How is one to become free from the bonds of work and therefore from rebirth? This is a vast topic and linked to the belief in reincarnation; simply put, karma is one's individual fate (as the certain consequences of actions done in previous lives); what happens to us in this life is the direct result of actions performed in other incarnations. Hence the importance of 'action under knowledge', a key theme in the *Gita* and *Upanishads*.

Kamala: lit. 'a lotus flower', 'rose-coloured or pale red', no doubt a reference to her lips. Her name is derived from Kama, the Hindu god of desire, sexual love. See e.g. Kama-Sutra.

Kamaswami: an invented name made up of Kama (see previous entry) and swami, 'master', owner, but more usually as a title to a monk or ascetic. The compound name therefore means in context 'a master in desire', and this sums up his role and function in the novel.

Krishna: Krishna and Rama are the two most famous earthly incarnations of Vishnu. Many legends surround the figure of Krishna as a great hero and teacher. In more recent legends he is often represented as a young and amorous flute-playing shepherd, the eighth son of Vasudeva.

Lakshmi: Goddess of beauty, prosperity and good luck. In later mythology often regarded as the wife of Vishnu or Narayana. Like Venus, she was born from the ocean's foam.

Magadha: In ancient India this was a kingdom near the present-day province of Bihar.

Mara: from the root 'mri', meaning killing or destroying (cf. English 'murder'). Hence the Evil One, the Destroyer, who tempts men to indulge their passions and is seen as the great enemy of Buddha and of his religion.

Maya: a Sanskrit term denoting illusion, the physical world of appearances that surrounds us, blinding us to the reality behind it. Maya is that power in Nature that creates this illusion. The work of spiritual aspirants is to seek and experience the unity behind apparent multiplicity.

Nirvana: from the root 'nirva', to blow out, extinguish. Hence, when all desires and passions are extinguished the highest bliss or beatitude, reunion with the Supreme Spirit, may be experienced.

Om: (Aum); whole books have been written on this sound! Simply; it appears in the *Upanishads* as a mystic monosyllable, the object of profound religious meditation. Later it came to represent the Hindu triad, Vishnu, Siva, Brahma. Om often begins and ends prayers, chants, meditations.

Prajapati: from Sanskrit prefix 'pra' plus root 'jan', to be born, produce, create, and 'pati', father, lord, etc. Hence the meaning, 'Lord of Creation, Protector of Life'.

Rig-Veda: the oldest of the Vedas (see under **Veda**).

Sakyamuni: a compound of 'sakya', the Buddha's family name and 'muni', sage, seer, saint. In the text the term is rendered as 'the wise man from the race of Sakya'.

Sansara: a Sanskrit term meaning 'circuit of mundane existence', metempsychosis, worldly illusion. What befalls Siddhartha when he leaves the Samanas aptly describes, in context, what Hesse intends to convey.

Samana: a variant of the Sanskrit 'sramana', to exert oneself, become weary, hence the meaning of performing 'acts of austerity', etc. Given in the text as 'wandering ascetics'. Its opposite is 'ashram', a place to rest, to retreat from the toils of this life and world.

Satyam: Sanskrit for 'true, real, pure', that which abides and exists beyond 'maya', illusion.

Savathi: at the time of Buddha the capital of Kosala, the present-day province of Oudh.

Self: one's innermost being, the 'embodied or individual self', as opposed to the small self or ego. As such the embodied self is a minute part of God Himself: it is this truth which is realized in self-realization, in the experience of unity. This is what both Govinda and Siddhartha seek.

Siddhartha: in Sanskrit a compound of 'siddha', acquired, accomplished, fulfilled, gained and of 'artha', aim, use, purpose, wealth, opulence; hence literally 'the wealth accrued to one who has fulfilled his aim'. The greatest wealth being self-realization.

Sutra: Sanskrit for 'thread', from 'siv', to sew ; see French 'suture'. Also 'that which runs through and holds things together'. Hence aphorisms, manuals, treatises, e.g. Dharma-sutras.

Sva-tantra: Sanskrit, literally meaning 'self or own' – 'system or model, class', etc. Hence that which has the system within itself. Compare, 'the kingdom of Heaven is within us'.

The Eight-Fold Path: following on from the Buddha's famous Four Noble Truths, a) that life is suffering, b) suffering results from desires, c) to stop suffering, stop desiring, d) to stop desiring there is the eight-fold path, which consists of 1) right views, 2) right intention, 3) right speech, 4) right action, 5) right livelihood, 6) right effort, 7) right awareness, 8) right concentration.

The Potter's Wheel: a very common image in Sanskritic texts; despite the diverse forms created by the potter, the substance is always one and the same; we return to our primeval source.

Übermensch: literally 'over – or super-man', both of which hardly do justice to the meaning implied by Nietzsche and therefore best left as it is. In context of Siddhartha, however, and as a guide, the sense is closer to our notion of 'hero'.

Upanishads: according to some 'the sitting down at the feet of another to listen to his words', hence secret knowledge given in this manner. But native authorities claim that the term means 'setting at rest ignorance by revealing the knowledge of the supreme spirit'. In the *Upanishads*, nothing is spoken of as a means to the attainment of the highest end of man except the knowledge of the identity of the self and Brahman; texts such as the Isha, Kena, and Brihadaranyaka are well worth our study. The novel mentions others.

Vasudeva: Name of the father of Krishna; the root 'vas' means to dwell or to shine' hence we may interpret his name as 'one in whom all things dwell or 'who dwells / shines in all things'.

Veda: from the root 'vid', to know; that body of sacred knowledge which constitutes the basis of the first period of the Hindu religion. Major texts are the Rig, Yajur and Sama Vedas.

Vedanta: see above. 'anta' means end, hence Vedanta either means the 'complete knowledge of the Vedas', or that which comes at the end of such writings, which are the *Upanishads*. The chief doctrine of Vedanta, as expounded by Shankara, is 'Advaita', the view that nothing really exists but the One Self or the Supreme Soul, Brahman.

Vishnu: The preserver as the second Godhead in the Hindu trinity. His name stems from the root 'vish', all-pervader. In many places today he is the most popular deity in Hindu worship.

Yoga-Veda: This does not exist as such. Did Hesse confuse it with Yoga-sutra? In the novel, he employs the term, however, with its original meaning of 'knowledge about the practices of yoga'.

Yoga: In Sanskrit, the root verb 'yuj' meaning to join, yoke, unite, connect, etc. has a plethora of uses. In context Siddhartha is concerned with the 'integration' which the practices of yoga bring about. These are the disciplines of the four paths of traditional yoga: bhakti (devotion), karma (action), jnana (knowledge), raja (meditation); strictly speaking, the purpose of all yogic practice is to concentrate the mind to obtain union with the Universal Spirit; hence those who think that yoga means 'asanas' (postures) and nothing else are mistaken. Yoga has eight limbs or aspects.

INDEX OF IMPORTANT PEOPLE AND WORKS MENTIONED

Bernoulli, Maria (1868–1963). Hesse's Swiss-born first wife, married in 1904, divorced 1923. Music – she loved singing – had drawn them together. An account of her 'mismarriage' is to be found in Hesse's novel *Rosshalde*, 1914. In a letter to his father, Hesse admits that the failure was due, not to a wrong choice, but rather to the inability of the 'artist' (i.e. himself) to marry.

Burckhardt, Jacob (1818–1892). Swiss historian and art historian, became increasingly interested in the new study of cultural history. Like Nietzsche he believed in aristocratic individualism. Major works include *Reflections on World History* and *The Culture of the Renaissance*. Hesse claims that Burckhardt was the 'third' greatest influence on him; the other two were home and India.

Dolbin, Ninón: née Auslander (1895–1966). Born in Rumania, loved art-history, folk-lore, and classical antiquity, became Hesse's third wife in 1931. A remarkably successful marriage, legacy of which is seen in their rich correspondence.

Freud, Sigmund (1856–1939). From its beginnings as a theory of neurosis, Freud developed psychoanalysis which offered Hesse fresh insights into the creative process and greatly influenced his constant search for the 'self'. In *Demian* and *Siddhartha*, especially, Freud's imprint is clear.

Goethe, Johannes, Wolfgang (1749–1832). The accepted genius of 'modern' Germany and a favourite author of Hesse's. Goethe has that rare distinction of having produced major works in all three literary genres: drama, prose, poetry. A truly astonishing individual who, seemingly, was interested in everything. For an introduction to his life and times the biography by Nicholas Boyle, Oxford, 1991, in two volumes, cannot be bettered.

Hölderlin, Friedrich (1770–1843). A Graecophile, who considered the poet as a visionary, *poeta vates*; his intense spirituality, seen best in his odes and elegies, would have appealed to Hesse. In nineteenth century Germany he was virtually 'unknown'; re-discovered by Stefan George in the twentieth century. His epistolary novel, *Hyperion* (1797), further exemplifies his major concerns as a writer.

Gustav Holst (1874–1934). English composer/teacher; his early work was strongly influenced by the poetry, mysticism and philosophy of the East. See his tone poem 'Indra' (1903); best known for his seven tone poems, *The Planets*. Holst also had an interest in Sanskrit.

Husserl, Edmund (1859–1938). Austrian philosopher who attempted to make philosophers examine 'Das Ding an sich' (the thing in itself). Known for his work on phenomenology, a major concern of his was the relationship between the pure ego and the 'life-world' (that is, our basic living experience), hence Hesse's 'interest' in him.

Lao-Tsu. Legendary Chinese philosopher of sixth century BC. Usually regarded as founder of Taoism (Tao means 'the way' and leads to the 'ultimate' or 'absolute'). His major work is *Tao te Ching*, his spiritual treatise on the way of Tao that has served China for centuries.

Messiaen, Olivier (1907–1992). French composer who described himself as a 'musical theologian'. He used a great variety of sources, e.g. Gregorian chants, Greek and Hindu 'ragas' (rhythms), composed for piano, organ, etc. Was Professor of Harmony at the Conservatoire in Paris.

Muktananda, Swami (1908–82). Born in Mangalore, South India, left home at fifteen to 'seek the truth'. Very similar to the life-story of Siddhartha, he wandered all over India, studied every doctrine, became an ascetic, and attained 'enlightenment' in 1956. Regarded as a saint by devotees, his major work, *Play of Consciousness*, bears comparison with Siddhartha.

Musil, Robert (1880–1942). Had an army education, then studied philosophy and became a freelance writer in 1922. Collected works run to 9 volumes; a prolific correspondent, his major work is the unfinished *The Man Without Qualities*, a witty encyclopaedia of life and history in pre-First World War Austria. Like Rilke, he has aroused considerable post-1945 critical attention.

Nietzsche, Friedrich (1844–1900). His philosophy was almost wholly neglected during his sane life, which came to a sudden end in 1889. Hesse was always intrigued by him and especially admired his aesthetic approach to life. With *Demian* and beyond, Nietzsche's views on morality, art, culture, the 'Outsider', etc. have visibly influenced Hesse in his writings. An excellent introduction to his life and works is the study by Michael Tanner.

Nityananda, Swami (?–1961). Legend surrounds his 'birth' but he is one of India's most revered modern saints and was the guru of Muktananda (see above). His story bears comparison with the 'lives' of Muktananda and Siddhartha, showing that *Siddhartha* is not 'escapist' literature.

Novalis, real name Friedrich von Hardenberg (1772–1801). Perhaps the most outstanding of German and European Romantics. A soul-mate of Hölderlin (see above), he was a 'visionary' in the true sense; his major works include *Hymnen an die Nacht* (*Hymns to the Night*, 1800). Exerted major influence on Hesse's writings, and is often mentioned in Hesse's correspondence.

Rilke, Rainer Maria (1875–1926). Born in Prague, he

led the life of a wanderer and yet became one of the most revered of European poets. Has aroused enormous post-war critical interest; major works include *Sonnets to Orpheus*, *The Book of Hours* and the *Duino Elegies*.

Schopenhauer, Arthur (1788–1860). The most readable of German philosophers, and a brilliant linguist. His work inspired many: Nietzsche, Freud, Wittgenstein and Hesse. His readings of Kant and Plato together with the *Upanishads* account for his radical insights into the unconscious, the nature of the self, individuality, mysticism, etc., all features of *Siddhartha*.

St-Exupéry, Antoine de (1900–1944). French pilot known for his exquisite novel *The Little Prince*. His views have a lot in common with those of Hesse, especially about war, the individual and the need for real spiritual values. His unfinished novel *Citadelle* concerns a new society of men, a theme very close to both Nietzsche and Hesse (cf. *The Glass Bead Game*)

Spengler, Oswald (1880–1936). Historian and political philosopher; predicted world-wide conflicts; was in favour of 'power politics'; his major work *The Decline of the West (1918–22)* only added to the doom and gloom of his epoch, thereby 'helping' Hesse to look eastwards for solutions.

Wenger, Ruth (1897–1980?). Hesse's second wife, the subject of several love-poems, was a singer. Married in 1924, marriage lasted eleven weeks only. Despite Hesse's frantic efforts at reconciliation, they were divorced in 1927. She became Ruth Haussman and moved to what became East Berlin.

Part One

The Brahmin's Son

In the shade of the house, in the sunshine on the river bank by the boats, in the shade of the sallow wood and the fig tree, Siddhartha, the handsome Brahmin's son, grew up with his friend Govinda. The sun browned his slender shoulders on the river bank, while bathing at the holy ablutions, at the holy sacrifices. Shadows passed across his eyes in the mango grove during play, while his mother sang, during his father's teachings, when with the learned men. Siddhartha had already long taken part in the learned men's conversations, had engaged in debate with Govinda and had practised the art of contemplation and meditation with him. Already he knew how to pronounce Om silently – this word of words, to say it inwardly with the intake of breath, when breathing out with all his soul, his brow radiating the glow of pure spirit. Already he knew how to recognize Atman within the depth of his being, indestructible, at one with the universe.

There was happiness in his father's heart because of his son who was intelligent and thirsty for knowledge; he saw him growing up to be a great learned man, a priest, a prince among Brahmins.

There was pride in his mother's breast when she saw

him walking, sitting down and rising; Siddhartha – strong, handsome, supple-limbed, greeting her with complete grace.

Love stirred in the hearts of the young Brahmins' daughters when Siddhartha walked through the streets of the town, with his lofty brow, his king-like eyes and his slim figure.

Govinda, his friend, the Brahmin's son, loved him more than anybody else. He loved Siddhartha's eyes and clear voice. He loved the way he walked, his complete grace of movement; he loved everything that Siddhartha did and said, and above all he loved his intellect, his fine ardent thoughts, his strong will, his high vocation. Govinda knew that he would not become an ordinary Brahmin, a lazy sacrificial official, an avaricious dealer in magic sayings, a conceited worthless orator, a wicked sly priest, or just a good stupid sheep amongst a large herd. No, and he, Govinda, did not want to become any of these, not a Brahmin like ten thousand others of their kind.

He wanted to follow Siddhartha, the beloved, the magnificent. And if he ever became a god, if he ever entered the All-Radiant, then Govinda wanted to follow him as his friend, his companion, his servant, his lance-bearer, his shadow.

That was how everybody loved Siddhartha. He delighted and made everybody happy.

But Siddhartha himself was not happy. Wandering along the rosy paths of the fig garden, sitting in contemplation in the bluish shade of the grove, washing his limbs in the daily bath of atonement, offering sacrifices in the depths of the shady mango wood with complete grace of manner, beloved by all, a joy to all, there was yet no joy in his own heart. Dreams and restless thoughts came flowing to him from the river, from the twinkling stars at night, from the sun's melting rays. Dreams and a restlessness of the soul came to him, arising from the smoke of the sacrifices, emanating from the verses of the Rig-Veda, trickling through from the teachings of the old Brahmins.

Siddhartha had begun to feel the seeds of discontent within him. He had begun to feel that the love of his father and mother, and also the love of his friend Govinda, would not always make him happy, give him peace, satisfy and suffice him. He had begun to suspect that his worthy father and his other teachers, the wise Brahmins, had already passed on to him the bulk and best of their wisdom, that they had already poured the sum total of their knowledge into his waiting vessel; and the vessel was not full, his intellect was not satisfied, his soul was not at peace, his heart was not still. The ablutions were good, but they were water; they did not wash sins away, they did not relieve the distressed heart. The sacrifices and the supplication of the gods were excellent – but were they everything? Did the sacrifices give happiness? And what about the gods? Was it really Prajapati who had created the world? Was it not Atman, He alone, who had created it? Were not the gods forms created like me and you, mortal, transient? Was it therefore good and right, was it a sensible and worthy act to offer sacrifices to the gods? To whom else should one offer sacrifices, to whom else should one pay honour, but to Him, Atman, the Only One? And where was Atman to be found, where did He dwell, where did His eternal heart beat, if not within the Self, in the innermost, in the eternal which each person carried within him? But where was this Self, this innermost? It was not flesh and bone, it was not thought or consciousness. That was what the wise men taught. Where, then, was it? To press towards the Self, towards Atman – was there another way that was worth seeking? Nobody showed the way, nobody knew it – neither his father, nor the teachers and wise men, nor the holy songs. The Brahmins and their holy books knew everything, everything: they had gone into everything – the creation of the world, the origin of speech, food, inhalation, exhalation, the arrangement of the senses, the acts of the gods. They knew a tremendous number of things – but was it worth while knowing all these things if they did not know the one important thing, the only important thing?

Many verses of the holy books, above all the Upanishads of Samaveda, spoke of this innermost thing. It is written: 'Your soul is the whole world.' It says that when a man is asleep, he penetrates his innermost and dwells in Atman. There was wonderful wisdom in these verses; all the knowledge of the sages was told here in enchanting language, pure as honey collected by the bees. No, this tremendous amount of knowledge, collected and preserved by successive generations of wise

Brahmins, could not be easily overlooked. But where were the Brahmins, the priests, the wise men, who were successful not only in having this most profound knowledge, but in experiencing it? Where were the initiated who, attaining Atman in sleep, could retain it in consciousness, in life, everywhere, in speech and in action? Siddhartha knew many worthy Brahmins, above all his father – holy, learned, of highest esteem. His father was worthy of admiration; his manner was quiet and noble. He lived a good life, his words were wise; fine and noble thoughts dwelt in his head – but even he who knew so much, did he live in bliss, was he at peace? Was he not also a seeker, insatiable? Did he not go continually to the holy springs with an insatiable thirst, to the sacrifices, to books, to the Brahmins' discourses? Why must he, the blameless one, wash away his sins and endeavour to cleanse himself anew each day? Was Atman then not within him? Was not then the source within his own heart? One must find the source within one's own Self, one must possess it. Everything else was seeking – a detour, error.

These were Siddhartha's thoughts; this was his thirst, his sorrow.

He often repeated to himself the words from one of the Chandogya-Upanishads. 'In truth, the name of the Brahman is Satyam. Indeed, he who knows it enters the heavenly world each day.' It often seemed near – the heavenly world – but never had he quite reached it, never had he quenched the final thirst. And among the wise men that he knew and whose teachings he enjoyed, there was not one who had entirely reached it – the heavenly world – not one who had completely quenched the eternal thirst.

'Govinda,' said Siddhartha to his friend, 'Govinda, come with me to the banyana tree. We will practise meditation.'

They went to the banyana tree and sat down, twenty paces apart. As he sat down ready to pronounce the Om, Siddhartha softly recited the verse:

> *'Om is the bow, the arrow is the soul,*
> *Brahman is the arrow's goal*
> *At which one aims unflinchingly.'*

When the customary time for the practice of meditation had passed, Govinda rose. It was now evening. It was time to perform the evening ablutions. He called Siddhartha by his name; he did not reply. Siddhartha sat absorbed, his eyes staring as if directed at a distant goal, the tip of his tongue showing a little between his teeth. He did not seem to be breathing. He sat thus, lost in meditation, thinking Om, his soul as the arrow directed at Brahman.

Some Samanas once passed through Siddhartha's town. Wandering ascetics, they were three thin worn-out men, neither old nor young, with dusty and bleeding shoulders, practically naked, scorched by the sun, solitary, strange and hostile – lean jackals in the world of men. Around them hovered an atmosphere of still passion, of devastating service, of unpitying self-denial.

In the evening, after the hour of contemplation, Siddhartha said to Govinda: 'Tomorrow morning my friend, Siddhartha is going to join the Samanas. He is going to become a Samana.'

Govinda blanched as he heard these words and read the decision in his friend's determined face, undeviating as the released arrow from the bow. Govinda realized from the first glance at his friend's face that now it was beginning. Siddhartha was going his own way; his destiny was beginning to unfold itself, and with his destiny, his own. And he became as pale as a dried banana skin.

'Oh, Siddhartha,' he cried, 'will your father permit it?'

Siddhartha looked at him like one who had just awakened. As quick as lightning he read Govinda's soul, read the anxiety, the resignation.

'We will not waste words, Govinda,' he said softly. 'Tomorrow at daybreak I will begin the life of the Samanas. Let us not discuss it again.'

Siddhartha went into the room where his father was sitting on a mat made of bast. He went up behind his father and remained standing there until his father felt his presence. 'Is it you, Siddhartha?' the Brahmin asked. 'Then speak what is in your mind.'

Siddhartha said: 'With your permission, Father, I have come to tell you that I wish to leave your house tomorrow and join the ascetics. I wish to become a Samana. I trust my father will not object.'

The Brahmin was silent so long that the stars passed across the small window and changed their design before the silence in the room was finally broken. His son stood silent and motionless with his arms folded. The father, silent and motionless, sat on the mat, and the stars passed across the sky. Then his father said: 'It is not seemly for Brahmins to utter forceful and angry words, but there is displeasure in my heart. I should not like to hear you make this request a second time.'

The Brahmin rose slowly. Siddhartha remained silent with folded arms.

'Why are you waiting?' asked his father.

'You know why,' answered Siddhartha.

His father left the room displeased and lay down on his bed.

As an hour passed by and he could not sleep, the Brahmin rose, wandered up and down and then left the house. He looked through the small window of the room and saw Siddhartha standing there with his arms folded, unmoving. He could see his pale robe shimmering. His heart troubled, the father returned to his bed.

As another hour passed and the Brahmin could not sleep, he rose again, walked up and down, left the house and saw the moon had risen. He looked through the window. Siddhartha stood there unmoving, his arms folded; the moon shone on his bare shinbones. His heart troubled, the father went to bed.

He returned again after an hour and again after two hours, looked through the window and saw Siddhartha standing there in the moonlight, in the starlight, in the dark. And he came silently again, hour after hour, looked into the room, and saw him standing unmoving. His heart filled with anger, with anxiety, with fear, with sorrow.

And in the last hour of the night, before daybreak, he returned again, entered the room and saw the youth standing there. He seemed tall and a stranger to him.

'Siddhartha,' he said, 'why are you waiting?'

'You know why.'

'Will you go on standing and waiting until it is day, noon, evening?'

'I will stand and wait.'

'You will grow tired, Siddhartha.'

'I will grow tired.'

'You will fall asleep, Siddhartha.'

'I will not fall asleep.'

'You will die, Siddhartha.'

'I will die.'

'And would you rather die than obey your father?'

'Siddhartha has always obeyed his father.'

'So you will give up your project?'

'Siddhartha will do what his father tells him.'

The first light of day entered the room. The Brahmin saw that Siddhartha's knees trembled slightly, but there was no trembling in Siddhartha's face; his eyes looked far away. Then the father realized that Siddhartha could no longer remain with him at home – that he had already left him.

The father touched Siddhartha's shoulder.

'You will go into the forest,' he said, 'and become a Samana. If you find bliss in the forest, come back and teach it to me. If you find disillusionment, come back, and we shall again offer sacrifices to the gods together. Now go, kiss your mother and tell her where you are going. For me, however, it is time to go to the river and perform the first ablution.'

He dropped his hand from his son's shoulder and went out. Siddhartha swayed as he tried to walk. He controlled himself, bowed to his father and went to his mother to do what had been told to him.

As, with benumbed legs, he slowly left the still sleeping town at daybreak, a crouching shadow emerged from the last hut and joined the pilgrim. It was Govinda.

'You have come,' said Siddhartha and smiled.

'I have come,' said Govinda.

With the Samanas

On the evening of that day they overtook the Samanas and requested their company and allegiance. They were accepted.

Siddhartha gave his clothes to a poor Brahmin on the road and only retained his loincloth and earth-coloured unstitched cloak. He only ate once a day and never cooked food. He fasted fourteen days. He fasted twenty-eight days. The flesh disappeared from his legs and cheeks. Strange dreams were reflected in his enlarged eyes. The nails grew long on his thin fingers and a dry, bristly beard appeared on his chin. His glance became icy when he encountered women; his lips curled with contempt when he passed through a town of well-dressed people. He saw businessmen trading, princes going to the hunt, mourners weeping over their dead, prostitutes offering themselves, doctors attending the sick, priests deciding the day for sowing, lovers making love, mothers soothing their children – and all were not worth a passing glance, everything lied, stank of lies; they were all illusions of sense, happiness and beauty. All were doomed to decay. The world tasted bitter. Life was pain.

Siddhartha had one single goal – to become empty,

to become empty of thirst, desire, dreams, pleasure and sorrow – to let the Self die. No longer to be Self, to experience the peace of an emptied heart, to experience pure thought – that was his goal. When all the Self was conquered and dead, when all passions and desires were silent, then the last must awaken, the innermost of Being that is no longer Self – the great secret!

Silently Siddhartha stood in the fierce sun's rays, filled with pain and thirst, and stood until he no longer felt pain and thirst. Silently he stood in the rain, water dripping from his hair on to his freezing shoulders, on to his freezing hips and legs. And the ascetic stood until his shoulders and legs no longer froze, till they were silent, till they were still. Silently he crouched among the thorns. Blood dripped from his smarting skin, ulcers formed, and Siddhartha remained stiff, motionless, till no more blood flowed, till there was no more pricking, no more smarting.

Siddhartha sat upright and learned to save his breath, to manage with little breathing, to hold his breath. He learned, while breathing in, to quiet his heartbeat, learned to lessen his heartbeats, until there were few and hardly any more.

Instructed by the eldest of the Samanas, Siddhartha practised self-denial and meditation according to the Samana rules. A heron flew over the bamboo wood and Siddhartha took the heron into his soul, flew over forest and mountains, became a heron, ate fishes, suffered heron hunger, used heron language, died a heron's death. A dead jackal lay on the sandy shore and

Siddhartha's soul slipped into its corpse; he became a dead jackal, lay on the shore, swelled, stank, decayed, was dismembered by hyenas, was picked at by vultures, became a skeleton, became dust, mingled with the atmosphere. And Siddhartha's soul returned, died, decayed, turned into dust, experienced the troubled course of the life cycle. He waited with new thirst like a hunter at a chasm where the life cycle ends, where there is an end to causes, where painless eternity begins. He killed his senses, he killed his memory, he slipped out of his Self in a thousand different forms. He was animal, carcass, stone, wood, water, and each time he reawakened. The sun or moon shone, he was again Self, swung into the life cycle, felt thirst, conquered thirst, felt new thirst.

Siddhartha learned a great deal from the Samanas; he learned many ways of losing the Self. He travelled along the path of self-denial through pain, through voluntary suffering and conquering of pain, through hunger, thirst and fatigue. He travelled the way of self-denial through meditation, through the emptying of the mind of all images. Along these and other paths did he learn to travel. He lost his Self a thousand times and for days on end he dwelt in non-being. But although the paths took him away from Self, in the end they always led back to it. Although Siddhartha fled from the Self a thousand times, dwelt in nothing, dwelt in animal and stone, the return was inevitable; the hour was inevitable when he would again find himself in sunshine or in moonlight, in shadow or in rain, and was again Self and Siddhartha, again felt the torment of the onerous life cycle.

At his side lived Govinda, his shadow; he travelled along the same path, made the same endeavours. They rarely conversed with each other apart from the necessities of their service and practices. Sometimes they went together through the villages in order to beg food for themselves and their teachers.

'What do you think, Govinda?' Siddhartha asked on one of these begging expeditions. 'Do you think we are any further? Have we reached our goal?'

Govinda replied: 'We have learned and we are still learning. You will become a great Samana, Siddhartha. You have learned each exercise quickly. The old Samanas have often praised you. Some day you will be a holy man, Siddhartha.'

Siddhartha said: 'It does not appear so to me, my friend. What I have so far learned from the Samanas I could have learned more quickly and easily in every inn in a prostitutes' quarter, amongst the carriers and dice players.'

Govinda said: 'Siddhartha is joking. How could you have learned meditation, holding of the breath and insensibility towards hunger and pain, with those wretches?'

And Siddhartha said softly, as if speaking to himself: 'What is meditation? What is abandonment of the body? What is fasting? What is the holding of breath? It is a flight from the Self, it is a temporary escape from the torment of Self. It is a temporary palliative against the pain and folly of life. The driver of oxen makes this same flight, takes this temporary drug when he drinks a few bowls of rice wine or coconut milk in the inn. He then no longer feels his Self, no longer feels the pain of life; he then experiences temporary escape. Falling asleep over his bowl of rice wine, he finds what Siddhartha and Govinda find when they escape from their bodies by long exercises and dwell in the non-Self.'

Govinda said: 'You speak thus, my friend, and yet you know that Siddhartha is no driver of oxen and a Samana is no drunkard. The drinker does indeed find escape, he does indeed find a short respite and rest, but he returns from the illusion and finds everything as it was before. He has not grown wiser, he has not gained knowledge, he has not climbed any higher.'

Siddhartha answered with a smile on his face: 'I do not know. I have never been a drunkard. But that I, Siddhartha, only find a short respite in my exercises and meditation, and am as remote from wisdom, from salvation, as a child in the womb, that, Govinda, I do know.'

On another occasion when Siddhartha left the wood with Govinda in order to beg for food for their brothers and teachers, Siddhartha began to speak and said: 'Well, Govinda, are we on the right road? Are we gaining knowledge? Are we approaching salvation? Or are we perhaps going in circles – we who thought to escape from the cycle?'

Govinda said: 'We have learned much, Siddhartha. There still remains much to learn. We are not going in circles, we are going upwards. The path is a spiral; we have already climbed many steps.'

Siddhartha replied: 'How old, do you think, is our oldest Samana, our worthy teacher?'

Govinda said: 'I think the eldest will be about sixty years old.'

And Siddhartha said: 'He is sixty years old and has not attained Nirvana. He will be seventy and eighty years old, and you and I, we shall grow as old as he, and do exercises and fast and meditate, but we will not attain Nirvana, neither he nor we. Govinda, I believe that amongst all the Samanas, probably not even one will attain Nirvana. We find consolations, we learn tricks with which we deceive ourselves, but the essential thing – the way – we do not find.'

'Do not utter such dreadful words, Siddhartha,' said Govinda. 'How could it be that amongst so many learned men, amongst so many Brahmins, amongst so many austere and worthy Samanas, amongst so many seekers, so many devoted to the inner life, so many holy men, none will find the right way?'

Siddhartha, however, said in a voice which contained as much grief as mockery, in a soft, somewhat sad, somewhat jesting voice: 'Soon, Govinda, your friend will leave the path of the Samanas along which he has travelled with you so long. I suffer thirst, Govinda, and on this long Samana path my thirst has not grown less. I have always thirsted for knowledge, I have always been full of questions. Year after year I have questioned the Brahmins, year after year I have questioned the holy

Vedas. Perhaps, Govinda, it would have been equally good, equally clever and holy, if I had questioned the rhinoceros or the chimpanzee. I have spent a long time and have not yet finished, in order to learn this, Govinda: that one can learn nothing. There is, so I believe, in the essence of everything, something that we cannot call learning. There is, my friend, only a knowledge – that is everywhere, that is Atman, that is in me and you and in every creature, and I am beginning to believe that this knowledge has no worse enemy than the man of knowledge, than learning.'

Thereupon Govinda stood still on the path, raised his hands and said: 'Siddhartha, do not distress your friend with such talk. Truly, your words trouble me. Think, what meaning would our holy prayers have, the venerableness of the Brahmins, the holiness of the Samanas, if, as you say, there is no learning? Siddhartha, what would become of everything, what would be holy on earth, what would be precious and sacred?'

Govinda murmured a verse to himself, a verse from one of the Upanishads:

'He whose reflective pure spirit sinks into Atman Knows bliss inexpressible through words.'

Siddhartha was silent. He dwelt long on the words which Govinda had uttered.

Yes, he thought, standing with bowed head, what

remains from all that seems holy to us? What remains? What is preserved? And he shook his head.

Once, when both youths had lived with the Samanas about three years and shared their practices, they heard from many sources a rumour, a report. Someone had appeared, called Gotama, the Illustrious, the Buddha. He had conquered in himself the sorrows of the world and had brought to a stand-still the cycle of rebirth. He wandered through the country preaching, sur-rounded by disciples, having no possessions, homeless, without a wife, wearing the yellow cloak of an ascetic, but with lofty brow, a holy man, and Brahmins and princes bowed before him and became his pupils.

This report, this rumour, this tale was heard and spread here and there. The Brahmins talked about it in the town, the Samanas in the forest. The name of Gotama, the Buddha, continually reached the ears of the young men, spoken of well and ill, in praise and in scorn.

Just as when a country is ravaged with the plague and rumour arises that there is a man, a wise man, a learned man, whose words and breath are sufficient to heal the afflicted, and as the report travels across the country and everyone speaks about it, many believe and many doubt it. Many, however, immediately go on their way to seek the wise man, the benefactor. In such a manner did that rumour, that happy report of Gotama the Buddha, the wise man from the race of Sakya, travel through the country. He possessed great knowledge, said the believers; he remembered his former lives, he had attained Nirvana and never returned on the cycle, he plunged no more into the troubled stream of forms. Many wonderful and incredible things were reported about him; he had performed wonders, had conquered the devil, had spoken with the gods. His enemies and doubters, however, said that this Gotama was an idle fraud; he passed his days in high living, scorned the sacrifices, was unlearned and knew neither practices nor mortification of the flesh.

The rumours of the Buddha sounded attractive; there was magic in these reports. The world was sick, life was difficult and here there seemed new hope, here there seemed to be a message, comforting, mild, full of fine promises. Everywhere there were rumours about the Buddha. Young men all over India listened, felt a longing and a hope. And among the Brahmins' sons in the towns and villages, every pilgrim and stranger was welcome if he brought news of him, the Illustrious, the Sakyamuni.

The rumours reached the Samanas in the forest and Siddhartha and Govinda, a little at a time, every little item heavy with hope, heavy with doubt. They spoke little about it, as the eldest Samana was no friend of this rumour. He had heard that this alleged Buddha had formerly been an ascetic and had lived in the woods, had then turned to high living and the pleasures of the world, and he held no brief for this Gotama.

'Siddhartha,' Govinda once said to his friend. 'Today I was in the village and a Brahmin invited me to enter his house and in the house was a Brahmin's son from

Magadha; he had seen the Buddha with his own eyes and had heard him preach. Truly I was filled with longing and I thought: I wish that both Siddhartha and I may live to see the day when we can hear the teachings from the lips of the Perfect One. My friend, shall we not also go hither and hear the teachings from the lips of the Buddha?'

Siddhartha said: 'I always thought that Govinda would remain with the Samanas. I always believed it was his goal to be sixty and seventy years old and still practise the arts and exercises which the Samanas teach. But how little did I know Govinda! How little did I know what was in his heart! Now, my dear friend, you wish to strike a new path and go and hear the Buddha's teachings.'

Govinda said: 'It gives you pleasure to mock me. No matter if you do, Siddhartha. Do you not also feel a longing, a desire to hear this teaching? And did you not once say to me – I will not travel the path of the Samanas much longer?'

Then Siddhartha laughed in such a way that his voice expressed a shade of sorrow and a shade of mockery and he said: 'You have spoken well, Govinda, you have remembered well, but you must also remember what else I told you – that I have become distrustful of teachings and learning and that I have little faith in words that come to us from teachers. But, very well, my friend, I am ready to hear that new teaching, although I believe in my heart that we have already tasted the best fruit of it.'

Govinda replied: 'I am delighted that you are agreed. But tell me, how can the teachings of the Gotama disclose to us its most precious fruit before we have even heard him?'

Siddhartha said: 'Let us enjoy this fruit and await further ones, Govinda. This fruit, for which we are already indebted to the Gotama, consists in the fact that he has enticed us away from the Samanas. Whether there are still other and better fruits, let us patiently await and see.'

On the same day, Siddhartha informed the eldest Samana of his decision to leave him. He told the old man with the politeness and modesty fitting to young men and students. But the old man was angry that both young men wished to leave him and he raised his voice and scolded them strongly.

Govinda was taken aback, but Siddhartha put his lips to Govinda's ear and whispered: 'Now I will show the old man that I have learnt something from him.'

He stood near the Samana, his mind intent; he looked into the old man's eyes and held him with his look, hypnotized him, made him mute, conquered his will, commanded him silently to do as he wished. The old man became silent, his eyes glazed, his will crippled; his arms hung down, he was powerless under Siddhartha's spell. Siddhartha's thoughts conquered those of the Samana; he had to perform what they commanded. And so the old man bowed several times, gave his blessings and stammered his wishes for a good journey.

The young men thanked him for his good wishes, returned his bow, and departed.

On the way, Govinda said: 'Siddhartha, you have learned more from the Samanas than I was aware. It is difficult, very difficult to hypnotize an old Samana. In truth, if you had stayed there, you would have soon learned how to walk on water.'

'I have no desire to walk on water,' said Siddhartha. 'Let the old Samanas satisfy themselves with such arts.'

Gotama

In the town of Savathi every child knew the name of the Illustrious Buddha and every house was ready to fill the alms-bowls of Gotama's silently begging disciples. Near the town was Gotama's favourite abode, the Jetavana grove, which the rich merchant Anathapindika, a great devotee of the Illustrious One, had presented to him and his followers.

The two young ascetics, in their search for Gotama's abode, had been referred to this district by tales and answers to their questions, and on their arrival at Savathi, food was offered to them immediately at the first house in front of whose door they stood silently begging. They partook of food and Siddhartha asked the lady who handed him the food:

'Good lady, we should very much like to know where the Buddha, the Illustrious One, dwells, for we are two Samanas from the forest and have come to see the Perfect One and hear his teachings from his own lips.'

The woman said: 'You have come to the right place, O Samanas from the forest. The Illustrious One sojourns in Jetavana, in the garden of Anathapindika. You may spend the night there, pilgrims, for there is enough room for the numerous people who flock there to hear the teachings from his lips.'

Then Govinda rejoiced and happily said: 'Ah, then we have reached our goal and our journey is at an end. But tell us, mother of pilgrims, do you know the Buddha? Have you seen him with your own eyes?'

The woman said: 'I have seen the Illustrious One many times. On many a day I have seen him walk through the streets, silently, in a yellow cloak, and silently hold out his alms-bowl at the house doors and return with his filled bowl.'

Govinda listened enchanted and wanted to ask many more questions and hear much more, but Siddhartha reminded him that it was time to go. They expressed their thanks and departed. It was hardly necessary to inquire the way, for quite a number of pilgrims and monks from Gotama's followers were on the way to Jetavana. When they arrived there at night, there were continual new arrivals. There was a stir of voices from them, requesting and obtaining shelter. The two Samanas, who were used to life in the forest, quickly and quietly found shelter and stayed there till morning.

At sunrise they were astounded to see the large number of believers and curious people who had spent the night there. Monks in yellow robes wandered along all the paths of the magnificent grove. Here and there they sat under the trees, lost in meditation or engaged in spirited talk. The shady gardens were like a town, swarming with bees. Most of the monks departed with their alms-bowls, in order to obtain food for their midday meal, the only one of the day. Even the Buddha himself went begging in the morning.

Siddhartha saw him and recognized him immediately, as if pointed out to him by a god. He saw him, bearing an alms-bowl, quietly leaving the place, an unassuming man in a yellow cowl.

'Look,' said Siddhartha softly to Govinda, 'there is the Buddha.'

Govinda looked attentively at the monk in the yellow cowl, who could not be distinguished in any way from the hundreds of other monks, and yet Govinda soon recognized him. Yes, it was he, and they followed him and watched him.

The Buddha went quietly on his way, lost in thought. His peaceful countenance was neither happy nor sad. He seemed to be smiling gently inwardly. With a secret smile, not unlike that of a healthy child, he walked along peacefully, quietly. He wore his gown and walked along exactly like the other monks, but his face and his step, his peaceful downward glance, his peaceful downward-hanging hand, and every finger of his hand spoke of peace, spoke of completeness, sought nothing, imitated nothing, reflected a continual quiet, an unfading light, an invulnerable peace.

And so Gotama wandered into the town to obtain alms, and the two Samanas recognized him only by his complete peacefulness of demeanour, by the stillness of his form, in which there was no seeking, no will, no counterfeit, no effort – only light and peace.

'Today we will hear the teachings from his own lips,' said Govinda.

Siddhartha did not reply. He was not very curious about the teachings. He did not think they would teach him anything new. He, as well as Govinda, had heard the substance of the Buddha's teachings, if only from second- and third-hand reports. But he looked attentively at Gotama's head, at his shoulders, at his feet, at his still, downward-hanging hand, and it seemed to him that in every joint of every finger of his hand there was knowledge; they spoke, breathed, radiated truth. This man, this Buddha, was truly a holy man to his finger tips. Never had Siddhartha esteemed a man so much, never had he loved a man so much.

They both followed the Buddha into the town and returned in silence. They themselves intended to abstain from food that day. They saw Gotama return, saw him take his meal within the circle of his disciples – what he ate would not have satisfied a bird – and saw him withdraw to the shades of the mango tree.

In the evening, however, when the heat abated and everyone in the camp was alert and gathered together, they heard the Buddha preach. They heard his voice, and this also was perfect, quiet and full of peace. Gotama talked about suffering, the origin of suffering, the way to release from suffering. Life was pain, the world was full of suffering, but the path to the release from suffering had been found. There was salvation for those who went the way of the Buddha.

The Illustrious One spoke in a soft but firm voice,

taught the four main points, taught the Eightfold Path; patiently he covered the usual method of teaching with examples and repetition. Clearly and quietly his voice was carried to his listeners – like a light, like a star in the heavens.

When the Buddha had finished – it was already night – many pilgrims came forward and asked to be accepted into the community, and the Buddha accepted them and said: 'You have listened well to the teachings. Join us then and walk in bliss; put an end to suffering.'

Govinda, the shy one, also stepped forward and said: 'I also wish to pay my allegiance to the Illustrious One and his teachings.' He asked to be taken into the community and was accepted.

As soon as the Buddha had withdrawn for the night, Govinda turned to Siddhartha and said eagerly: 'Siddhartha, it is not for me to reproach you. We have both listened to the Illustrious One, we have both heard his teachings. Govinda has listened to the teachings and has accepted them, but you my dear friend, will you not also tread the path of salvation? Will you delay, will you still wait?'

When he heard Govinda's words, Siddhartha awakened as if from a sleep. He looked at Govinda's face for a long time. Then he spoke softly and there was no mockery in his voice. 'Govinda, my friend, you have taken the step, you have chosen your path. You have always been my friend, Govinda, you have always gone a step behind me. Often I have thought: will Govinda ever take a step without me, from his own conviction?

Now, you are a man and have chosen your own path. May you go along it to the end, my friend. May you find salvation!'

Govinda, who did not yet fully understand, repeated his question impatiently: 'Speak, my dear friend, say that you also cannot do other than swear allegiance to the Buddha.'

Siddhartha placed his hand on Govinda's shoulder. 'You have heard my blessing, Govinda. I repeat it. May you travel this path to the end. May you find salvation!'

In that moment, Govinda realized that his friend was leaving him and he began to weep.

'Siddhartha,' he cried.

Siddhartha spoke kindly to him. 'Do not forget, Govinda, that you now belong to the Buddha's holy men. You have renounced home and parents, you have renounced origin and property, you have renounced your own will, you have renounced friendship. That is what the teachings preach, that is the will of the Illustrious One. That is what you wished yourself. Tomorrow, Govinda, I will leave you.'

For a long time the friends wandered through the woods. They lay down for a long time but could not sleep. Govinda pressed his friend again and again to tell him why he would not follow the Buddha's teachings, what flaw he found in them, but each time Siddhartha waved him off: 'Be at peace, Govinda. The Illustrious One's teachings are very good. How could I find a flaw in them?'

Early in the morning, one of the Buddha's followers,

one of his oldest monks, went through the garden and called to him all the new people who had sworn their allegiance to the teachings, in order to place upon them the yellow robe and instruct them in the first teachings and duties of their order. Thereupon Govinda tore himself away, embraced the friend of his youth, and drew on the monk's robe.

Siddhartha wandered through the grove deep in thought.

There he met Gotama, the Illustrious One, and as he greeted him respectfully and the Buddha's expression was so full of goodness and peace, the young man plucked up courage and asked the Illustrious One's permission to speak to him. Silently the Illustrious One nodded his permission.

Siddhartha said: 'Yesterday, O Illustrious One, I had the pleasure of hearing your wonderful teachings. I came from afar with my friend to hear you, and now my friend will remain with you; he has sworn allegiance to you. I, however, am continuing my pilgrimage anew.'

'As you wish,' said the Illustrious One politely.

'My talk is perhaps too bold,' continued Siddhartha, 'but I do not wish to leave the Illustrious One without sincerely communicating to him my thoughts. Will the Illustrious One hear me a little longer?'

Silently the Buddha nodded his consent.

Siddhartha said: 'O Illustrious One, in one thing above all have I admired your teachings. Everything is completely clear and proved. You show the world as a complete, unbroken chain, an eternal chain, linked together by cause and effect. Never has it been presented so clearly, never has it been so irrefutably demonstrated. Surely every Brahmin's heart must beat more quickly, when through your teachings he looks at the world, completely coherent, without a loophole, clear as crystal, not dependent on chance, not dependent on the gods. Whether it is good or evil, whether life in itself is pain or pleasure, whether it is uncertain – that it may perhaps be this is not important – but the unity of the world, the coherence of all events, the embracing of the big and the small from the same stream, from the same law of cause, of becoming and dying: this shines clearly from your exalted teachings, O Perfect One. But according to your teachings, this unity and logical consequence of all things is broken in one place. Through a small gap there streams into the world of unity something strange, something new, something that was not there before and that cannot be demonstrated and proved: that is your doctrine of rising above the world, of salvation. With this small gap, through this small break, however, the eternal and single world law breaks down again. Forgive me if I raise this objection.'

Gotama had listened quietly, motionless. And now the Perfect One spoke in his kind, polite and clear voice. 'You have listened well to the teachings, O Brahmin's son, and it is a credit to you that you have thought so deeply about them. You have found a flaw. Think well about it again. Let me warn you, you who are thirsty for knowledge, against the thicket of opinions and the conflict of words. Opinions mean nothing; they may be beautiful or ugly, clever or foolish, anyone can embrace or reject them. The teaching which you have heard, however, is not my opinion, and its goal is not to explain the world to those who are thirsty for knowledge. Its goal is quite different; its goal is salvation from suffering. That is what Gotama teaches, nothing else.'

'Do not be angry with me, O Illustrious One,' said the young man. 'I have not spoken to you thus to quarrel with you about words. You are right when you say that opinions mean little, but may I say one thing more? I did not doubt you for one moment. Not for one moment did I doubt that you were the Buddha, that you have reached the highest goal which so many thousands of Brahmins and Brahmin's sons are striving to reach. You have done so by your own seeking in your own way, through thought, through meditation, through knowledge, through enlightenment. You have learned nothing through teachings, and so I think, O Illustrious One, that nobody finds salvation through teachings. To nobody, O Illustrious One, can you communicate in words and teachings, what happened to you in the hour of your enlightenment. The teachings of the enlightened Buddha embrace much, they teach much – how to live righteously, how to avoid evil. But there is one thing that this clear, worthy instruction does not contain; it does not contain the secret of what the Illustrious One himself experienced – he alone among hundreds of thousands. That is what I thought and realized when I heard your teachings. That is why I am going on my way – not to seek another and better doctrine, for I know there is none, but to leave all doctrines and all teachers and to reach my goal alone – or die. But I will often remember this day, O Illustrious One, and this hour when my eyes beheld a holy man.'

The Buddha's eyes were lowered, his unfathomable face expressed complete equanimity.

'I hope you are not mistaken in your reasoning,' said the Illustrious One slowly. 'May you reach your goal! But tell me, have you seen my gathering of holy men, my many brothers who have sworn allegiance to the teachings? Do you think, O Samana from afar, that it would be better for all these to relinquish the teachings and to return to the life of the world and desires?'

'That thought never occurred to me,' cried Siddhartha. 'May they all follow the teachings! May they reach their goal! It is not for me to judge another life. I must judge for myself. I must choose and reject. We Samanas seek release from the Self, O Illustrious One. If I were one of your followers, I fear that it would only be on the surface, that I would deceive myself that I was at peace and had attained salvation, while in truth the Self would continue to live and grow, for it would have been transformed into your teachings, into my allegiance and love for you and for the community of the monks.'

Half smiling, with imperturbable brightness and

friendliness, the Buddha looked steadily at the stranger and dismissed him with a hardly visible gesture.

'You are clever, O Samana,' said the Illustrious One; 'you know how to speak cleverly, my friend. Be on your guard against too much cleverness.'

The Buddha walked away and his look and half-smile remained imprinted in Siddhartha's memory for ever. I have never seen a man look and smile, sit and walk like that, he thought. I, also, would like to look and smile, sit and walk like that, so free, so worthy, so restrained, so candid, so childlike and mysterious. A man only looks and walks like that when he has conquered his Self. I also will conquer my Self.

I have seen one man, one man only, thought Siddhartha, before whom I must lower my eyes. I will never lower my eyes before any other man. No other teachings will attract me, since this man's teachings have not done so.

The Buddha has robbed me, thought Siddhartha. He has robbed me, yet he has given me something of greater value. He has robbed me of my friend, who believed in me and who now believes in him; he was my shadow and is now Gotama's shadow. But he has given to me Siddhartha, myself.

Awakening

As Siddhartha left the grove in which the Buddha, the Perfect One, remained, in which Govinda remained, he felt that he had also left his former life behind him in the grove. As he slowly went on his way, his head was full of this thought. He reflected deeply, until this feeling completely overwhelmed him and he reached a point where he recognized causes; for to recognize causes, it seemed to him, is to think, and through thought alone feelings become knowledge and are not lost, but become real and begin to mature.

Siddhartha reflected deeply as he went on his way. He realized that he was no longer a youth; he was now a man. He realized that something had left him, like the old skin that a snake sheds. Something was no longer in him, something that had accompanied him right through his youth and was part of him: this was the desire to have teachers and to listen to their teachings. He had left the last teacher he had met, even he, the greatest and wisest teacher, the holiest, the Buddha. He had to leave him; he could not accept his teachings.

Slowly the thinker went on his way and asked himself: what is it that you wanted to learn from teachings and teachers, and although they taught you much, what was it they could not teach you? And he thought: It was the Self, the character and nature of which I wished to learn. I wanted to rid myself of the Self, to conquer it, but I could not conquer it, I could only deceive it, could only fly from it, could only hide from it. Truly, nothing in the world has occupied my thoughts as much as the Self, this riddle, that I live, that I am one and am separated and different from everybody else, that I am Siddhartha; and about nothing in the world do I know less than about myself, about Siddhartha.

The thinker, slowly going on his way, suddenly stood still, gripped by this thought, and another thought immediately arose from this one. It was: The reason why I do not know anything about myself, the reason why Siddhartha has remained alien and unknown to myself is due to one thing, to one single thing – I was afraid of myself, I was fleeing from myself. I was seeking Brahman, Atman, I wished to destroy myself, to get away from myself, in order to find in the unknown innermost, the nucleus of all things, Atman, Life, the Divine, the Absolute. But by doing so, I lost myself on the way.

Siddhartha looked up and around him, a smile crept over his face, and a strong feeling of awakening from a long dream spread right through his being. Immediately he walked on again, quickly, like a man who knows what he has to do.

Yes, he thought, breathing deeply, I will no longer try to escape from Siddhartha. I will no longer devote my thoughts to Atman and the sorrows of the world. I will no longer mutilate and destroy myself in order to find a secret behind the ruins. I will no longer study Yoga-Veda, Atharva-Veda, or asceticism, or any other teachings. I will learn from myself, be my own pupil; I will learn from myself the secret of Siddhartha.

He looked around him as if seeing the world for the first time. The world was beautiful, strange and mysterious. Here was blue, here was yellow, here was green, sky and river, woods and mountains, all beautiful, all mysterious and enchanting, and in the midst of it, he, Siddhartha, the awakened one, on the way to himself. All this, all this yellow and blue, river and wood, passed for the first time across Siddhartha's eyes. It was no longer the magic of Mara, it was no more the veil of Maya, it was no longer meaningless and the chance diversities of the appearances of the world, despised by deep-thinking Brahmins, who scorned diversity, who sought unity. River was river, and if the One and Divine in Siddhartha secretly lived in blue and river, it was just the divine art and intention that there should be yellow and blue, there sky and wood – and here Siddhartha. Meaning and reality were not hidden somewhere behind things, they were in them, in all of them.

How deaf and stupid I have been, he thought, walking on quickly. When anyone reads anything which he wishes to study, he does not despise the letters and punctuation marks, and call them illusion, chance and worthless shells, but he reads them, he studies and loves them, letter by letter. But I, who wished to read the book of the world and the book of my own nature, did presume to despise the letters and signs. I called the world of appearances, illusion. I called my eyes and tongue, chance. Now it is over; I have awakened. I have indeed awakened and have only been born today.

But as these thoughts passed through Siddhartha's mind, he suddenly stood still, as if a snake lay in his path.

Then suddenly this also was clear to him: he, who was in fact like one who had awakened or was newly born, must begin his life completely afresh. When he left the Jetavana grove that morning, the grove of the Illustrious One, already awakened, already on the way to himself, it was his intention and it seemed the natural course for him after the years of his asceticism to return to his home and his father. Now, however, in that moment as he stood still, as if a snake lay in his path, this thought also came to him: I am no longer what I was, I am no longer an ascetic, no longer a priest, no longer a Brahmin. What then shall I do at home with my father? Study? Offer sacrifices? Practise meditation? All this is over for me now.

Siddhartha stood still and for a moment an icy chill stole over him. He shivered inwardly like a small animal, like a bird or hare, when he realized how alone he was. He had been homeless for years and had not felt like this. Now he did feel it. Previously, when in deepest meditation, he was still his father's son, he was a Brahmin of high standing, a religious man. Now he was only Siddhartha, the awakened; otherwise nothing else. He breathed in deeply and for a moment he shuddered. Nobody was so alone as he. He was no nobleman, belonging to any aristocracy, no artisan belonging to any guild and finding refuge in it, sharing its life and language. He was no Brahmin, sharing the life of the Brahmins, no ascetic belonging to the Samanas. Even the most secluded hermit in the woods was not one and alone; he also belonged to a class of people. Govinda had become a monk and thousands of monks were his brothers, wore the same gown, shared his beliefs and spoke his language. But he, Siddhartha, where did he belong? Whose life would he share? Whose language would he speak?

At that moment, when the world around him melted away, when he stood alone like a star in the heavens, he was overwhelmed by a feeling of icy despair, but he was more firmly himself than ever. That was the last shudder of his awakening, the last pains of birth. Immediately he moved on again and began to walk quickly and impatiently, no longer homewards, no longer to his father, no longer looking backwards.

Part Two

Kamala

Siddhartha learned something new on every step of his path, for the world was transformed and he was enthralled. He saw the sun rise over forest and mountains and set over the distant palm shore. At night he saw the stars in the heavens and the sickle-shaped moon floating like a boat in the blue. He saw trees, stars, animals, clouds, rainbows, rocks, weeds, flowers, brook and river, the sparkle of dew on bushes in the morning, distant high mountains blue and pale; birds sang, bees hummed, the wind blew gently across the rice fields. All this, coloured and in a thousand different forms, had always been there. The sun and moon had always shone; the rivers had always flowed and the bees had hummed, but in previous times all this had been nothing to Siddhartha but a fleeting and illusive veil before his eyes, regarded with distrust, condemned to be disregarded and ostracized from the thoughts, because it was not reality, because reality lay on the other side of the visible. But now his eyes lingered on this side; he saw and recognized the visible and he sought his place in this world. He did not seek reality; his goal was not on any other side. The world was beautiful when looked at in this way – without any seeking, so simple, so childlike. The moon and the stars were beautiful, the brook, the shore, the forest and rock, the goat and the golden beetle, the flower and butterfly were beautiful. It was beautiful and pleasant to go through the world like that, so childlike, so awakened, so concerned with the immediate, without any distrust. Elsewhere the sun burned fiercely, elsewhere there was cool in the forest shade; elsewhere there were pumpkins and bananas. The days and nights were short, every hour passed quickly like a sail on the sea, beneath the sail of a ship full of treasures, full of joy. Siddhartha saw a group of monkeys in the depths of the forest, moving about high in the branches, and heard their wild eager cries. Siddhartha saw a ram follow a sheep and mate. In a lake of rushes he saw the pike making chase in evening hunger. Swarms of young fishes, fluttering and glistening, moved anxiously away from it. Strength and desire were reflected in the swiftly moving whirls of water by the raging pursuer.

All this had always been and he had never seen it; he was never present. Now he was present and belonged to it. Through his eyes he saw light and shadows; through his mind he was aware of moon and stars.

On the way, Siddhartha remembered all that he had experienced in the garden of Jetavana, the teachings that he had heard there from the holy Buddha, the parting from Govinda and the conversation with the Illustrious One. He remembered each word that he had said to the Illustrious One, and he was astonished that he had said things which he did not then really know.

What he had said to the Buddha – that the Buddha's wisdom and secret was not teachable, that it was inexpressible and incommunicable – and which he had once experienced in an hour of enlightenment, was just what he had now set off to experience, what he was now beginning to experience. He must gain experience himself. He had known for a long time that his Self was Atman, of the same eternal nature as Brahman, but he had never really found his Self, because he had wanted to trap it in the net of thoughts. The body was certainly not the Self, nor the play of senses, nor thought, nor understanding, nor acquired wisdom or art with which to draw conclusions and from already existing thoughts to spin new thoughts. No, this world of thought was still on this side, and it led to no goal when one destroyed the senses of the incidental Self but fed it with thoughts and erudition. Both thought and the senses were fine things, behind both of them lay hidden the last meaning; it was worth while listening to them both, to play with both, neither to despise nor overrate either of them, but to listen intently to both voices. He would only strive after whatever the inward voice commanded him, not tarry anywhere but where the voice advised him. Why did Gotama once sit down beneath the bo tree in his greatest hour when he received enlightenment? He had heard a voice, a voice in his own heart which commanded him to seek rest under this tree, and he had not taken recourse to mortification of the flesh, sacrifices, bathings or prayers, eating or drinking, sleeping or dreaming; he had listened to the voice. To obey no other external command, only the voice, to be prepared – that was good, that was necessary. Nothing else was necessary.

During the night, as he slept in a ferryman's straw hut, Siddhartha had a dream. He dreamt that Govinda stood before him, in the yellow robe of the ascetic. Govinda looked sad and asked him, 'Why did you leave me?' Thereupon he embraced Govinda, put his arm round him, and as he drew him to his breast and kissed him, he was Govinda no longer, but a woman and out of the woman's gown emerged a full breast, and Siddhartha lay there and drank; sweet and strong tasted the milk from this breast. It tasted of woman and man, of sun and forest, of animal and flower, of every fruit, of every pleasure. It was intoxicating. When Siddhartha awoke, the pale river shimmered past the door of the hut, and in the forest the cry of an owl rang out, deep and clear.

As the day began, Siddhartha asked his host, the ferryman, to take him across the river. The ferryman took him across on his bamboo raft. The broad sheet of water glimmered pink in the light of the morning.

'It is a beautiful river,' he said to his companion.

'Yes,' said the ferryman, 'it is a very beautiful river. I love it above everything. I have often listened to it, gazed at it, and I have always learned something from it. One can learn much from a river.'

'Thank you, good man,' said Siddhartha, as he landed on the other side. 'I am afraid I have no gift to give you, nor any payment. I am homeless, a Brahmin's son and a Samana.'

'I could see that,' said the ferryman, 'and I did not expect any payment or gift from you. You will give it to me some other time.'

'Do you think so?' asked Siddhartha merrily.

'Certainly. I have learned that from the river too; everything comes back. You, too, Samana, will come back. Now farewell, may your friendship be my payment! May you think of me when you sacrifice to the gods!'

Smiling, they parted from each other. Siddhartha was pleased at the ferryman's friendliness. He is like Govinda, he thought, smiling. All whom I meet on the way are like Govinda. All are grateful, although they themselves deserve thanks. All are subservient, all wish to be my friend, to obey and to think little. People are children.

At midday he passed through a village. Children danced about in the lane in front of the clay huts. They played with pumpkin-stones and mussels. They shouted and wrestled with each other, but ran away timidly when the strange Samana appeared. At the end of the village, the path went alongside a brook, and at the edge of the brook a young woman was kneeling and washing clothes. When Siddhartha greeted her, she raised her head and looked at him with a smile, so that he could see the whites of her eyes shining. He called across a benediction, as is customary among travellers, and asked how far the road still was to the large town.

Thereupon she stood up and came towards him, her moist lips gleaming attractively in her young face. She exchanged light remarks with him, asked him if he had yet eaten, and whether it was true that the Samanas slept alone in the forest at night and were not allowed to have any women with them. She then placed her left foot on his right and made a gesture, such as a woman makes when she invites a man to that kind of enjoyment of love which the holy books call 'ascending the tree'. Siddhartha felt his blood kindle, and as he recognized his dream again at that moment, he stooped a little towards the woman and kissed the brown tip of her breast. Looking up he saw her face smiling, full of desire, and her half-closed eyes pleading with longing.

Siddhartha also felt a longing and the stir of sex in him but as he had never yet touched a woman, he hesitated a moment, although his hands were ready to seize her. At that moment he heard his inward voice and the voice said 'No!' Then all the magic disappeared from the young woman's smiling face; he saw nothing but the ardent glance of a passionate young woman. Gently he stroked her cheek and quickly disappeared from the disappointed woman into the bamboo wood.

Before evening of that day he reached a large town and he was glad, because he had a desire to be with people. He had lived in the woods for a long time and the ferryman's straw hut, in which he had slept the previous night, was the first roof he had had over him for a long time.

Outside the town, by a beautiful unfenced grove, the

wanderer met a small train of men and women servants loaded with baskets. In the middle, in an ornamented sedan chair carried by four people, sat a woman, the mistress, on red cushions beneath a coloured awning. Siddhartha stood still at the entrance to the grove and watched the procession, the men servants, the maids and the baskets. He looked at the sedan chair and the lady in it. Beneath heaped-up black hair he saw a bright, very sweet, very clever face, a bright red mouth like a freshly cut fig, artful eyebrows painted in a high arch, dark eyes, clever and observant, and a clear slender neck above her green and gold gown. The woman's hands were firm and smooth, long and slender, with broad gold bangles on her wrists.

Siddhartha saw how beautiful she was and his heart rejoiced. He bowed low as the sedan chair passed close by him, and raising himself again, gazed at the bright fair face, and for a moment into the clever arched eyes, and inhaled the fragrance of a perfume which he did not recognize.

For a moment the beautiful woman nodded and smiled, then disappeared into the grove, followed by her servants.

And so, thought Siddhartha, I enter this town under a lucky star. He felt the urge to enter the grove immediately, but he thought it over, for it had just occurred to him how the men servants and maids had looked at him at the entrance, so scornfully, so distrustfully, so dismissing in their glance.

I am still a Samana, he thought, still an ascetic and

a beggar. I cannot remain one. I cannot enter the grove like this. And he laughed.

He inquired from the first people that he met about the grove and the woman's name, and learned that it was the grove of Kamala, the well-known courtesan, and that besides the grove she owned a house in the town.

Then he entered the town. He had only one goal. Pursuing it, he surveyed the town, wandered about in the maze of streets, stood still in places, and rested on the stone steps to the river.

Towards evening he made friends with a barber's assistant, whom he had seen working in the shade of an arch. He found him again at prayer in the temple of Vishnus, where he related to him stories about Vishnus and Lakshmi. During the night he slept among the boats on the river, and early in the morning, before the first customers arrived in the shop, he had his beard shaved off by the barber's assistant. He also had his hair combed and rubbed with fine oil. Then he went to bathe in the river.

When the beautiful Kamala was approaching her grove late in the afternoon in her sedan chair, Siddhartha was at the entrance. He bowed and received the courtesan's greeting. He beckoned the servant who was last in the procession, and asked him to announce to his mistress that a young Brahmin desired to speak to her. After a time the servant returned, asked Siddhartha to follow him, conducted him silently into a pavilion, where Kamala lay on a couch, and left him.

'Did you not stand outside yesterday and greet me?' asked Kamala.

'Yes indeed. I saw you yesterday and greeted you.'

'But did you not have a beard and long hair yesterday, and dust in your hair?'

'You have observed well, you have seen everything. You have seen Siddhartha, the Brahmin's son, who left his home in order to become a Samana, and who was a Samana for three years. Now, however, I have left that path and have come to this town, and the first person I met before I reached the town was you. I have come here to tell you, O Kamala, that you are the first woman to whom Siddhartha has spoken without lowered eyes. Never again will I lower my eyes when I meet a beautiful woman.'

Kamala smiled and played with her fan made of peacocks' feathers, and asked, 'Is that all that Siddhartha has come to tell me?'

'I have come to tell you this and to thank you because you are so beautiful. And if it does not displease you, Kamala, I would like to ask you to be my friend and teacher, for I do not know anything of the art of which you are mistress.'

Thereupon Kamala laughed aloud.

'It has never been my experience that a Samana from the woods should come to me and desire to learn from me. Never has a Samana with long hair and an old torn loincloth come to me. Many young men come to me, including Brahmins' sons, but they come to me in fine clothes, in fine shoes; there is scent in their hair

121

and money in their purses. That is how these young men come to me, O Samana.'

Siddhartha said: 'I am already beginning to learn from you. I already learned something yesterday. Already I have got rid of my beard, I have combed and oiled my hair. There is not much more that is lacking, most excellent lady: fine clothes, fine shoes and money in my purse. Siddhartha has undertaken to achieve more difficult things than these trifles and has attained them. Why should I not attain what I decided to undertake yesterday? – to be your friend and to learn the pleasures of love from you. You will find me an apt pupil, Kamala. I have learned more difficult things than what you have to teach me. So Siddhartha is not good enough for you as he is, with oil in his hair, but without clothes, without shoes and without money!'

Kamala laughed and said: 'No, he is not yet good enough. He must have clothes, fine clothes, and shoes, fine shoes, and plenty of money in his purse and presents for Kamala. Do you know now, Samana from the woods? Do you understand?'

'I understand very well,' cried Siddhartha. 'How could I fail to understand when it comes from such a mouth? Your mouth is like a freshly cut fig, Kamala. My lips are also red and fresh, and will fit yours well, you will see. But tell me, fair Kamala, are you not at all afraid of the Samana from the forest, who has come to learn about love?'

'Why should I be afraid of a Samana, a stupid

Samana from the forest, who comes from the jackals and does not know anything about women?'

'Oh, the Samana is strong and afraid of nothing. He could force you, fair maiden, he could rob you, he could hurt you.'

'No, Samana, I am not afraid. Has a Samana or a Brahmin ever feared that someone could come and strike him and rob him of his knowledge, of his piety, of his power for depth of thought? No, because they belong to himself, and he can only give of them what he wishes, and if he wishes. That is exactly how it is with Kamala and with the pleasures of love. Fair and red are Kamala's lips, but try to kiss them against Kamala's will, and not one drop of sweetness will you obtain from them – although they know well how to give sweetness. You are an apt pupil, Siddhartha, so learn also this. One can beg, buy, be presented with and find love in the streets, but it can never be stolen. You have misunderstood. Yes, it would be a pity if a fine young man like you misunderstood.'

Siddhartha bowed and smiled. 'You are right, Kamala, it would be a pity. It would be a very great pity. No, no drops of sweetness must be lost from your lips, nor from mine. So Siddhartha will come again when he has what he is lacking in – clothes, shoes, money. But tell me, fair Kamala, can you not give me a little advice?'

'Advice? Why not? Who would not willingly give advice to a poor, ignorant Samana who comes from the jackals in the forest?'

'Dear Kamala, where can I go in order to obtain these three things as quickly as possible?'

'My friend, many people want to know that. You must do what you have learned and obtain money, clothes and shoes for it. A poor man cannot obtain money otherwise.'

'I can think, I can wait, I can fast.'

'Nothing else?'

'Nothing. O yes, I can compose poetry. Will you give me a kiss for a poem?'

'I will do so if your poem pleases me. What is it called?'

After thinking a moment, Siddhartha recited this verse:

'Into her grove went the fair Kamala,
At the entrance to the grove stood the brown Samana.
As he saw the lotus flower,
Deeply he bowed.
Smiling, acknowledged Kamala,
Better, thought the young Samana,
To make sacrifices to the fair Kamala
Than to offer sacrifices to the gods.'

Kamala clapped her hands loudly, so that the golden bangles tinkled.

'Your poetry is very good, brown Samana, and truly there is nothing to lose if I give you a kiss for it.'

She drew him to her with her eyes. He put his face against hers, placed his lips against hers, which were like a freshly cut fig. Kamala kissed him deeply, and to Siddhartha's great excitement he felt how much she taught him, how clever she was, how she mastered him, repulsed him, lured him, and how after this long kiss, a long series of other kisses, all different, awaited him. He stood still, breathing deeply. At that moment he was like a child astonished at the fullness of knowledge and learning which unfolded itself before his eyes.

'Your poetry is very good,' said Kamala. 'If I were rich I would give you money for it. But it will be hard for you to earn as much money as you want with poetry. For you will need much money if you want to be Kamala's friend.'

'How you can kiss, Kamala!' stammered Siddhartha.

'Yes, indeed, that is why I am not lacking in clothes, shoes, bangles and all sorts of pretty things. But what are you going to do? Cannot you do anything else besides think, fast and compose poetry?'

'I also know the sacrificial songs,' said Siddhartha, 'but I will not sing them any more. I also know incantations but I will not pronounce them any more. I have read the scriptures . . .'

'Wait,' interrupted Kamala, 'you can read and write.'

'Certainly I can. Many people can do that.'

'Not most people. I cannot. It is very good that you know how to read and write, very good. You might even need the incantations.'

At that moment a servant entered and whispered something in his mistress's ear.

'I have a visitor,' said Kamala. 'Hurry and disappear,

125

Siddhartha, nobody must see you here. I will see you again tomorrow.'

However, she ordered the servant to give the holy Brahmin a white gown. Without quite knowing what was happening, Siddhartha was led away by the servant, conducted by a circuitous route to a garden house, presented with a gown, let into the thicket and expressly instructed to leave the grove unseen, as quickly as possible.

Contentedly, he did what he was told. Accustomed to the forest, he made his way silently out of the grove and over the hedge. Contentedly, he returned to the town, carrying his rolled-up gown under his arm. He stood at the door of an inn where travellers met, silently begged for food and silently accepted a piece of rice cake. Perhaps tomorrow, he thought, I will not need to beg for food.

He was suddenly overwhelmed with a feeling of pride. He was a Samana no longer; it was no longer fitting that he should beg.

He gave the rice cake to a dog and remained without food.

The life that is lived here is simple, thought Siddhartha. It has no difficulties. Everything was difficult, irksome and finally hopeless when I was a Samana. Now everything is easy, as easy as the instruction in kissing which Kamala gives. I require clothes and money, that is all. These are easy goals which do not disturb one's sleep.

He had long since inquired about Kamala's town house and called there the next day.

'Things are going well,' she called across to him. 'Kamaswami expects you to call on him; he is the richest merchant in the town. If you please him, he will take you into his service. Be clever, brown Samana! I had your name mentioned to him through others. Be friendly towards him; he is very powerful, but do not be too modest. I do not want you to be his servant, but his equal, otherwise I shall not be pleased with you. Kamaswami is beginning to grow old and indolent. If you please him, he will place great confidence in you.'

Siddhartha thanked her and laughed, and when she learned that he had not eaten that day nor the previous day, she ordered bread and fruit to be brought to him and attended him.

'You have been lucky,' she said to him on parting; 'one door after the other is being opened to you. How does that come about? Have you a charm?'

Siddhartha said: 'Yesterday I told you I knew how to think, to wait and to fast, but you did not consider these useful. But you will see that they are very useful, Kamala. You will see that the stupid Samanas in the forest learn and know many useful things. The day before yesterday I was still an unkempt beggar; yesterday I already kissed Kamala and soon I will be a merchant and have money and all those things which you value.'

'Quite,' she agreed, 'but how would you have fared

without me? Where would you be if Kamala did not help you?'

'My dear Kamala,' said Siddhartha, 'when I came to you in your grove I made the first step. It was my intention to learn about love from the most beautiful woman. From the moment I made that resolution I also knew that I would execute it. I knew that you would help me; I knew it from your first glance at the entrance to the grove.'

'And if I had not wanted?'

'But you did want. Listen, Kamala, when you throw a stone into the water, it finds the quickest way to the bottom of the water. It is the same when Siddhartha has an aim, a goal. Siddhartha does nothing; he waits, he thinks, he fasts, but he goes through the affairs of the world like the stone through water, without doing anything, without bestirring himself; he is drawn and lets himself fall. He is drawn by his goal, for he does not allow anything to enter his mind which opposes his goal. That is what Siddhartha learned from the Samanas. It is what fools call magic and what they think is caused by demons. Nothing is caused by demons; there are no demons. Everyone can perform magic, everyone can reach his goal, if he can think, wait and fast.'

Kamala listened to him. She loved his voice, she loved the look in his eyes.

'Perhaps it is as you say, my friend,' she said softly, 'and perhaps it is also because Siddhartha is a handsome man, because his glance pleases women, that he is lucky.'

Siddhartha kissed her and said goodbye. 'May it be so, my teacher. May my glance always please you, may good fortune always come to me from you!'

Amongst the People

Siddhartha went to see Kamaswami, the merchant, and was shown into a rich house. Servants conducted him across costly carpets to a room where he waited for the master of the house.

Kamaswami came in, a supple, lively man, with greying hair, with clever prudent eyes and a sensual mouth. Master and visitor greeted each other in a friendly manner.

'I have been told,' the merchant began, 'that you are a Brahmin, a learned man, but that you seek service with a merchant. Are you then in need, Brahmin, that you seek service?'

'No,' replied Siddhartha, 'I am not in need and I have never been in need. I have come from the Samanas with whom I lived for a long time.'

'If you come from the Samanas, how is that you are not in need? Are not all the Samanas completely without possessions?'

'I possess nothing,' said Siddhartha, 'if that is what you mean. I am certainly without possessions, but of my own free will, so I am not in need.'

'But how will you live if you are without possessions?'

'I have never thought about it, sir. I have been without possessions for nearly three years and I have never thought on what I should live.'

'So you have lived on the possessions of others?'

'Apparently. The merchant also lives on the possessions of others.'

'Well spoken, but he does not take from others for nothing, he gives his goods in exchange.'

'That seems to be the way of things. Everyone takes, everyone gives. Life is like that.'

'Ah, but if you are without possessions, how can you give?'

'Everyone gives what he has. The soldier gives strength, the merchant goods, the teacher instruction, the farmer rice, the fisherman fish.'

'Very well and what can you give? What have you learned that you can give?'

'I can think, I can wait, I can fast.'

'Is that all?'

'I think that is all.'

'And of what use are they? For example, fasting, what good is that?'

'It is of great value, sir. If a man has nothing to eat, fasting is the most intelligent thing he can do. If, for instance, Siddhartha had not learned how to fast, he would have had to seek some kind of work today, either with you, or elsewhere, for hunger would have driven him. But as it is, Siddhartha can wait calmly. He is not impatient, he is not in need, he can ward off hunger for a long time and laugh at it. Therefore, fasting is useful, sir.'

'You are right, Samana. Wait a moment.'

Kamaswami went out and returned with a roll which he handed to his guest and inquired: 'Can you read this?'

Siddhartha looked at the roll, on which a sales agreement was written, and began to read the contents.

'Excellent,' said Kamaswami, 'and will you write something for me on this sheet?'

He gave him a sheet and a pen and Siddhartha wrote something and returned the sheet.

Kamaswami read: 'Writing is good, thinking is better. Cleverness is good, patience is better.'

'You write very well,' the merchant praised him. 'We shall still have plenty to discuss, but today I invite you to be my guest and to live in my house.'

Siddhartha thanked him and accepted. He now lived in the merchant's house. Clothes and shoes were brought to him and a servant prepared him a bath daily. Splendid meals were served twice a day, but Siddhartha only ate once a day, and neither ate meat nor drank wine. Kamaswami talked to him about his business, showed him goods and warehouses and accounts. Siddhartha learned many new things; he heard much and said little. And remembering Kamala's words, he was never servile to the merchant, but compelled him to treat him as an equal and even more than his equal. Kamaswami conducted his business with care and often with passion, but Siddhartha regarded it all as a game, the rules of which he endeavoured to learn well, but which did not stir his heart.

He was not long in Kamaswami's house when he was already taking a part in his master's business. Daily, however, at the hour she invited him, he visited the beautiful Kamala, in handsome clothes, in fine shoes, and soon he also brought her presents. He learned many things from her wise red lips. Her smooth gentle hand taught him many things. He, who was still a boy as regards love and was inclined to plunge to the depths of it blindly and insatiably, was taught by her that one cannot have pleasure without giving it, and that every gesture, every caress, every touch, every glance, every single part of the body has its secret which can give pleasure to one who can understand.

She taught him that lovers should not separate from each other after making love without admiring each other, without being conquered as well as conquering, so that no feeling of satiation or desolation arises nor the horrid feeling of misusing or having been misused. He spent wonderful hours with the clever, beautiful courtesan and became her pupil, her lover, her friend. Here with Kamala lay the value and meaning of his present life, not in Kamaswami's business.

The merchant passed on to him the writing of important letters and orders, and grew accustomed to conferring with him about all important affairs. He soon saw that Siddhartha understood little about rice and wool, shipping and trading, but that he had a happy knack and surpassed the merchant in calmness and equanimity, and in the art of listening and making a good impression on strange people. 'This Brahmin,' he said to a friend, 'is no real merchant and will never be one; he is never absorbed in the business. But he has the secret of those people to whom success comes by itself, whether it is due to being born under a lucky star or whether it is magic, or whether he has learned it from the Samanas. He always seems to be playing at business, it never makes much impression on him, it never masters him, he never fears failure, he is never worried about a loss.'

The friend advised the merchant: 'Give him a third of the profits of the business which he conducts for you, but let him share the same proportion of losses if any arise. He will thus become more enthusastic.'

Kamaswami followed his advice, but Siddhartha was little concerned about it. If he made a profit, he accepted it calmly; if he suffered a loss, he laughed and said, 'Oh, well, this transaction has gone badly.'

He did, in fact, seem indifferent about business. Once he travelled to a village in order to buy a large rice harvest. When he arrived there, the rice was already sold to another merchant. However, Siddhartha remained in that village several days, entertained the farmers, gave money to the children, attended a wedding and returned from the journey completely satisfied. Kamaswami reproached him for not returning immediately, for wasting time and money. Siddhartha replied: 'Do not scold, my dear friend. Nothing was ever achieved by scolding. If a loss has been sustained,

I will bear the loss. I am very satisfied with this journey. I have become acquainted with many people, I have become friendly with a Brahmin, children have sat on my knee, farmers have showed me their fields. Nobody took me for a merchant.'

'That is all very fine,' admitted Kamaswami reluctantly, 'but you are in fact a merchant. Or were you only travelling for your pleasure?'

'Certainly I travelled for my pleasure,' laughed Siddhartha. 'Why not? I have become acquainted with people and new districts. I have enjoyed friendship and confidence. Now, if I had been Kamaswami, I should have departed immediately feeling very annoyed when I saw I was unable to make a purchase, and time and money would indeed have been lost. But I spent a number of good days, learned much, had much pleasure and did not hurt either myself or others through annoyance or hastiness. If I ever go there again, perhaps to buy a later harvest, or for some other purpose, friendly people will receive me and I will be glad that I did not previously display hastiness and displeasure. Anyway, let it rest, my friend, and do not hurt yourself by scolding. If the day comes when you think, this Siddhartha is doing me harm, just say one word and Siddhartha will go on his way. Until then, however, let us be good friends.'

The merchant's attempts to convince Siddhartha that he was eating his, Kamaswami's, bread were also in vain. Siddhartha ate his own bread; moreover, they all ate the bread of others, everybody's bread. Siddhartha was never concerned about Kamaswami's troubles and Kamaswami had many troubles. If a transaction threatened to be unsuccessful, if a consignment of goods was lost, if a debtor appeared unable to pay, Kamaswami could never persuade his colleague that it served any purpose to utter troubled or angry words, to form wrinkles on the forehead and sleep badly. When Kamaswami once reminded him that he had learned everything from him, he replied: 'Do not make such jokes. I have learned from you how much a basket of fish costs and how much interest one can claim for lending money. That is your knowledge. But I did not learn how to think from you, my dear Kamaswami. It would be better if you learned that from me.'

His heart was not indeed in business. It was useful in order to bring him money for Kamala, and it brought him more than he really needed. Moreover, Siddhartha's sympathy and curiosity lay only with people, whose work, troubles, pleasures and follies were more unknown and remote from him than the moon. Although he found it so easy to speak to everyone, to live with everyone, to learn from everyone, he was very conscious of the fact that there was something which separated him from them – and this was due to the fact that he had been a Samana. He saw people living in a childish or animal-like way, which he both loved and despised. He saw them toiling, saw them suffer and grow grey about things that to him did not seem worth the price – for money, small pleasures and trivial honours. He saw them scold and hurt each other; he saw them lament over pains at which the Samana laughs, and suffer at deprivations which a Samana does not feel.

He accepted all that people brought to him. The merchant who brought him linen for sale was welcome; the debtor who sought a loan was welcome, the beggar was welcome who stayed an hour telling him the story of his poverty, and who was yet not as poor as any Samana. He did not treat the rich foreign merchant differently from the servant who shaved him and the pedlars from whom he bought bananas and let himself be robbed of small coins. If Kamaswami came to him and told him his troubles or made him reproaches about a transaction, he listened curiously and attentively, was amazed at him, tried to understand him, conceded to him a little where it seemed necessary and turned away from him to the next one who wanted him. And many people came to him – many to trade with him, many to deceive him, many to listen to him, many to elicit his sympathy, many to listen to his advice. He gave advice, he sympathized, he gave presents, he allowed himself to be cheated a little, and he occupied his thoughts with all this game and the passion with which all men play it, as much as he had previously occupied his thoughts with the gods and Brahman.

At times he heard within him a soft, gentle voice, which reminded him quietly, complained quietly, so that he could hardly hear it. Then he suddenly saw clearly that he was leading a strange life, that he was doing many things that were only a game, that he was quite cheerful and sometimes experienced pleasure, but that real life was flowing past him and did not touch him. Like a player who plays with his ball, he played with his business, with the people around him, watched them, derived amusement from them; but with his heart, with his real nature, he was not there. His real self wandered elsewhere, far away, wandered on and on invisibly and had nothing to do with his life.

He was sometimes afraid of these thoughts and wished that he could also share their childish daily affairs with intensity, truly to take part in them, to enjoy and live their lives instead of only being there as an onlooker.

He visited the beautiful Kamala regularly, learned the art of love in which, more than anything else, giving and taking become one. He talked to her, learned from her, gave her advice, received advice. She understood him better than Govinda had once done. She was more like him.

Once he said to her: 'You are like me; you are different from other people. You are Kamala and no one else, and within you there is a stillness and sanctuary to which you can retreat at any time and be yourself, just as I can. Few people have that capacity and yet everyone could have it.'

'Not all people are clever,' said Kamala.

'It has nothing to do with that, Kamala,' said Siddhartha. 'Kamaswami is just as clever as I am and yet he has no sanctuary. Others have it who are only children in understanding. Most people, Kamala, are like a falling leaf that drifts and turns in the air, flutters, and falls to the ground. But a few others are like stars which travel one defined path: no wind reaches them, they have within themselves their guide and path. Among all the wise men, of whom I knew many, there was one who was perfect in this respect. I can never forget him. He is Gotama, the Illustrious One who preaches this gospel. Thousands of young men hear his teachings every day and follow his instructions every hour, but they are all falling leaves; they have not the wisdom and guide within themselves.'

Kamala looked at him and smiled. 'You are talking about him again,' she said. 'Again you have Samana thoughts.'

Siddhartha was silent, and they played the game of love, one of the thirty or forty different games which Kamala knew. Her body was as supple as a jaguar and a hunter's bow; whoever learned about love from her, learned many pleasures, many secrets. She played with Siddhartha for a long time, repulsed him, overwhelmed him, conquered him, rejoiced at her mastery, until he was overcome and lay exhausted at her side.

The courtesan bent over him and looked long at his face, into his eyes that had grown tired.

'You are the best lover that I have had,' she said thoughtfully. 'You are stronger than others, more supple, more willing. You have learned my art well. Siddhartha. Some day, when I am older, I will have a child by you. And yet, my dear, you have remained a Samana. You do not really love me – you love nobody. Is that not true?'

'Maybe,' said Siddhartha wearily. 'I am like you. You cannot love either, otherwise how could you practise love as an art? Perhaps people like us cannot love. Ordinary people can – that is their secret.'

Sansara

For a long time Siddhartha had lived the life of the world without belonging to it. His senses, which he had deadened during his ardent Samana years, were again awakened. He had tasted riches, passion and power, but for a long time he remained a Samana in his heart. Clever Kamala had recognized this. His life was always directed by the art of thinking, waiting and fasting. The people of the world, the ordinary people, were still alien to him, just as he was apart from them.

The years passed by. Enveloped by comfortable circumstances, Siddhartha hardly noticed their passing. He had become rich. He had long possessed a house of his own and his own servants, and a garden on the outskirts of the town, by the river. People liked him, they came to him if they wanted money or advice. However, with the exception of Kamala, he had no close friends.

That glorious, exalted awakening which he had once experienced in his youth, in the days after Gotama's preaching, after the parting from Govinda, that alert expectation, that pride of standing alone without teachers and doctrines, that eager readiness to hear the divine voice within his own heart had gradually become a memory, had passed. The holy fountainhead which had once been near and which had once sung loudly within him, now murmured softly in the distance. However, many things which he had learned from the Samanas, which he had learned from Gotama, from his father, from the Brahmins, he still retained for a long time: a moderate life, pleasure in thinking, hours of meditation, secret knowledge of the Self, of the eternal Self, that was neither body nor consciousness. Many of these he had retained; others were submerged and covered with dust. Just as the potter's wheel, once set into motion, still turns for a long time and then turns only very slowly and stops, so did the wheel of the ascetic, the wheel of thinking, the wheel of discrimination still revolve for a long time in Siddhartha's soul; it still revolved, but slowly and hesitatingly, and it had nearly come to a standstill. Slowly, like moisture entering the dying tree trunk, slowly filling and rotting it, so did the world and inertia creep into Siddhartha's soul; it slowly filled his soul, made it heavy, made it tired, sent it to sleep. But on the other hand his senses became more awakened, they learned a great deal, experienced a great deal.

Siddhartha had learned how to transact business affairs, to exercise power over people, to amuse himself with women; he had learned to wear fine clothes, to command servants, to bathe in sweet-smelling waters. He had learned to eat sweet and carefully prepared foods, also fish and meat and fowl, spices and dainties, and to drink wine which made him lazy and forgetful.

He had learned to play dice and chess, to watch dancers, to be carried in sedan chairs, to sleep on a soft bed. But he had always felt different from and superior to the others; he had always watched them a little scornfully, with a slightly mocking disdain, with that disdain which a Samana always feels towards the people of the world. If Kamaswami was upset, if he felt that he had been insulted, or if he was troubled with business affairs, Siddhartha had always regarded him mockingly. But slowly and imperceptibly, with the passing of the seasons, his mockery and feeling of superiority diminished. Gradually, along with his growing riches, Siddhartha himself acquired some of the characteristics of the ordinary people, some of their childishness and some of their anxiety. And yet he envied them; the more he became like them, the more he envied them. He envied them the one thing that he lacked and that they had: the sense of importance with which they had lived their lives, the depth of their pleasures and sorrows, the anxious but sweet happiness of their continual power to love. These people were always in love with themselves, with their children, with honour or money, with plans or hope. But these he did not learn from them, these childlike pleasures and follies; he only learned the unpleasant things from them which he despised. It happened more frequently that after a merry evening, he lay late in bed the following morning and felt dull and tired. He would become annoyed and impatient when Kamaswami bored him with his worries. He would laugh too loudly when he lost at dice. His face was still more clever and intellectual than other people's, but he rarely laughed, and gradually his face assumed the expressions which are so often found among rich people – the expressions of discontent, of sickliness, of displeasure, of idleness, of lovelessness. Slowly the soul sickness of the rich crept over him.

Like a veil, like a thin mist, a weariness settled on Siddhartha, slowly, every day a little thicker, every month a little darker, every year a little heavier. As a new dress grows old with time, loses its bright colour, becomes stained and creased, the hems frayed, and here and there weak and threadbare places, so had Siddhartha's new life which he had begun after his parting from Govinda, become old. In the same way it lost its colour and sheen with the passing of the years: creases and stains accumulated and, hidden in the depths, here and there already appearing, waited disillusionment and nausea. Siddhartha did not notice it. He only noticed that the bright and clear inward voice, that had once awakened in him and had always guided him in his finest hours, had become silent.

The world had caught him; pleasure, covetousness, idleness, and finally also the vice that he had always despised and scorned as the most foolish – acquisitiveness. Property, possessions and riches had also finally trapped him. They were no longer a game and a toy; they had become a chain and a burden. Siddhartha wandered along a strange, twisted path of this last and most base declivity through the game of dice. Since the time he had stopped being a Samana in his heart, Siddhartha began to play dice for money and jewels with increasing fervour, a game in which he had previously smilingly and indulgently taken part as a custom of the ordinary people. He was a formidable player; few dared play with him for his stakes were so high and reckless. He played the game as a result of a heartfelt need. He derived a passionate pleasure through the gambling away and squandering of wretched money. In no other way could he show more clearly and mockingly his contempt for riches, the false deity of businessmen. So he staked high and unsparingly, hating himself, mocking himself. He won thousands, he threw thousands away, lost money, lost jewels, lost a country house, won again, lost again. He loved that anxiety, that terrible and oppressive anxiety which he experienced during the game of dice, during the suspense of high stakes. He loved this feeling and continually sought to renew it, to increase it, to stimulate it, for in this feeling alone did he experience some kind of happiness, some kind of excitement, some heightened living in the midst of his satiated, tepid, insipid existence. And after every great loss he devoted himself to the procurement of new riches, went eagerly after business and pressed his debtors for payment, for he wanted to play again, he wanted to squander again, he wanted to show his contempt for riches again. Siddhartha became impatient at losses, he lost his patience with slow-paying debtors, he was no longer kindhearted to beggars, he no longer had the desire to give gifts and loans to the poor. He, who staked ten thousand on the throw of the dice and laughed, became more hard and mean in business, and sometimes dreamt of money at night. And whenever he awakened from this hateful spell, when he saw his face reflected in the mirror on the wall of his bedroom, grown older and uglier, whenever shame and nausea overtook him, he fled again, fled to a new game of chance, fled in confusion to passion, to wine, and from there back again to the urge for acquiring and hoarding wealth. He wore himself out in this senseless cycle, became old and sick.

Then a dream reminded him. He had been with Kamala in the evening, in her lovely pleasure garden. They sat under a tree talking. Kamala was speaking seriously, and grief and weariness were concealed behind her words. She had asked him to tell her about Gotama, and could not hear enough about him, how clear his eyes were, how peaceful and beautiful his mouth, how gracious his smile, how peaceful his entire manner. For a long time he had to talk to her about the Illustrious Buddha and Kamala had sighed and said: 'One day, perhaps soon, I will also become a follower of this Buddha. I will give him my pleasure garden and take refuge in his teachings.' But then she enticed him, and in love play she clasped him to her with extreme fervour, fiercely and tearfully, as if she wanted once more to extract the last sweet drop from this fleeting pleasure. Never had it been so strangely clear to Siddhartha how closely related passion was to death. Then he lay beside her and Kamala's face was near to his, and under her eyes and near the corners of her mouth he read clearly for the first time a sad sign – fine lines and wrinkles, a sign which gave a reminder of autumn and old age. Siddhartha himself, who was only in his forties, had noticed grey hairs here and there in his black hair. Weariness was written on Kamala's beautiful face, weariness from continuing along a path which had no joyous goal, weariness and incipient old age and, concealed and not yet mentioned, perhaps a not yet conscious fear – fear of the autumn of life, fear of old age, fear of death. Sighing, he took leave of her, his heart full of misery and secret fear.

Then Siddhartha had spent the night at his house with dancers and wine, had pretended to be superior to his companions, which he no longer was. He had drunk much wine and later after midnight he went to bed, tired and yet agitated, nearly in tears and in despair. In vain did he try to sleep. His heart was so full of misery, he felt he could no longer endure it. He was full of nausea which overpowered him like a distasteful wine, or music that was too sweet and superficial, or like the too sweet smile of the dancers or the too sweet perfume of their hair and breasts. But above all he was nauseated with himself, with his perfumed hair, with the smell of wine from his mouth, with the soft, flabby appearance of his skin. Like one who has eaten and drunk too much and vomits painfully and then feels better, so did the restless man wish he could rid himself with one terrific heave of these pleasures, of these habits, of this entirely senseless life.

Only at daybreak and at the first signs of activity outside his town house did he doze off and had a few moments of semi-oblivion, a possibility of sleep. During that time he had a dream.

Kamala kept a small rare songbird in a small golden cage. It was about this bird that he dreamt. This bird, which usually sang in the morning, became mute, and as this surprised him, he went up to the cage and looked inside. The little bird was dead and lay stiff on the floor. He took it out, held it a moment in his hand and then threw it away on the road, and at the same moment he was horrified and his heart ached as if he had thrown away with this dead bird all that was good and of value in himself.

Awakening from this dream, he was overwhelmed by a feeling of great sadness. It seemed to him that he had spent his life in a worthless and senseless manner; he retained nothing vital, nothing in any way precious or worth while. He stood alone, like a shipwrecked man on the shore.

Sadly, Siddhartha went to a pleasure garden that belonged to him, closed the gates, sat under a mango tree, and felt horror and death in his heart. Gradually, he collected his thoughts and mentally went through the whole of his life, from the earliest days which he could remember. When had he really been happy? When had he really experienced joy? Well, he had experienced this several times. He had tasted it in the days of his boyhood, when he had won praise from the Brahmins, when he far outstripped his contemporaries, when he excelled himself at the recitation of the holy verses, in argument with the learned men, when assisting at the sacrifices. Then he had felt in his heart: 'A path lies before you which you are called to follow. The gods await you.' And again as a youth when his continually soaring goal had propelled him in and out of the crowd of similar seekers, when he had striven hard to understand the Brahmins' teachings, when every freshly acquired knowledge only engendered a new thirst, then again, in the midst of his thirst, in the midst of his efforts, he had thought: Onwards, onwards, this is your path. He had heard this voice when he had left his home and chosen the life of the Samanas, and again when he had left the Samanas and gone to the Perfect One, and also when he left him for the unknown. How long was it now since he had heard this voice, since he had soared to any heights? How flat and desolate his path had been! How many long years he had spent without any lofty goal, without any thirst, without any exaltation, content with small pleasures and yet never really satisfied! Without knowing it, he had endeavoured and longed all these years to be like all these other people, like these children, and yet his life had been much more wretched and poorer than theirs, for their aims were not his, nor their sorrows his. This whole world of the Kamaswami people had only been a game to him, a dance, a comedy which one watches. Only Kamala was dear to him – had been of value to him – but was she still? Did he still need her – and did she still need him? Were they not playing a game without an end? Was it necessary to live for it? No. This game was called Sansara, a game for children, a game which was perhaps enjoyable played once, twice, ten times – but was it worth playing continually?

Then Siddhartha knew that the game was finished, that he could play it no longer. A shudder passed through his body; he felt as if something had died.

He sat all that day under the mango tree, thinking of his father, thinking of Govinda, thinking of Gotama. Had he left all these in order to become a Kamaswami?

He sat there till night fell. When he looked up and saw the stars, he thought: I am sitting here under my mango tree, in my pleasure garden. He smiled a little. Was it necessary, was it right, was it not a foolish thing that he should possess a mango tree and a garden?

He had finished with that. That also died in him. He rose, said farewell to the mango tree and the pleasure garden. As he had not had any food that day he felt extremely hungry, and thought of his house in the town, of his room and bed, of the table with food. He smiled wearily, shook his head and said goodbye to these things.

The same night Siddhartha left his garden and the town and never returned. For a long time Kamaswami tried to find him, believing he had fallen into the hands of bandits. Kamala did not try to find him. She was not surprised when she learned that Siddhartha had disappeared. Had she not always expected it? Was he not a Samana, without a home, a pilgrim? She had felt it more than ever at their last meeting, and in the midst of her pain at her loss, she rejoiced that she had pressed him so close to her heart on that last occasion, had felt so completely possessed and mastered by him.

When she heard the first news of Siddhartha's disappearance, she went to the window where she kept a rare song-bird in a golden cage. She opened the door of the cage, took the bird out and let it fly away. For a long time she looked after the disappearing bird. From that day she received no more visitors and kept her house closed. After a time, she found that she was with child as a result of her last meeting with Siddhartha.

By the River

Siddhartha wandered into the forest, already far from the town and knew only one thing – that he could not go back, that the life he had lived for many years was past, tasted and drained to a degree of nausea. The songbird was dead; its death, which he had dreamt about, was the bird in his own heart. He was deeply entangled in Sansara, he had drawn nausea and death to himself from all sides, like a sponge that absorbs water until it is full. He was full of ennui, full of misery, full of death; there was nothing left in the world that could attract him, that could give him pleasure and solace.

He wished passionately for oblivion, to be at rest, to be dead. If only a flash of lightning would strike him! If only a tiger would come and eat him! If there were only some wine, some poison, that would give him oblivion, that would make him forget, that would make him sleep and never awaken! Was there any kind of filth with which he had not besmirched himself, any sin and folly which he had not committed, any stain upon his soul for which he alone had not been responsible? Was it then still possible to live? Was it possible to take in breath again and again, to breathe out, to feel hunger, to eat again, to sleep again, to lie with women again? Was this cycle not exhausted and finished for him?

Siddhartha reached the long river in the wood, the same river across which a ferryman had once taken him when he was still a young man and had come from Gotama's town. He stopped at this river and stood hesitatingly on the bank. Fatigue and hunger had weakened him. Why should he go any farther, where, and for what purpose? There was no more purpose, there was nothing more than a deep, painful longing to shake off this whole confused dream, to spit out this stale wine, to make an end of this bitter, painful life.

There was a tree on the river bank, a coconut tree. Siddhartha leaned against it, placed his arm round the trunk and looked down into the green water which flowed beneath him. He looked down and was completely filled with a desire to let himself go and be submerged in the water. A chilly emptiness in the water reflected the terrible emptiness in his soul. Yes, he was at the end. There was nothing more for him but to efface himself, to destroy the unsuccessful structure of his life, to throw it away, mocked at by the gods. That was the deed which he longed to commit, to destroy the form which he hated! Might the fishes devour him, this dog of a Siddhartha, this madman, this corrupted and rotting body, this sluggish and misused soul! Might the fishes and crocodiles devour him, might the demons tear him to little pieces!

With a distorted countenance he stared into the water. He saw his face reflected, and spat at it; he took his arm away from the tree trunk and turned a little, so that he could fall headlong and finally go under. He bent, with closed eyes – towards death.

Then from a remote part of his soul, from the past of his tired life, he heard a sound. It was one word, one syllable, which without thinking he spoke indistinctly, the ancient beginning and ending of all Brahmin prayers, the holy Om, which had the meaning of 'the Perfect One' or 'Perfection'. At that moment, when the sound of Om reached Siddhartha's ears, his slumbering soul suddenly awakened and he recognized the folly of his action.

Siddhartha was deeply horrified. So that was what he had come to; he was so lost, so confused, so devoid of all reason, that he had sought death. This wish, this childish wish had grown so strong within him: to find peace by destroying his body. All the torment of those recent times, all the disillusionment, all the despair, had not affected him so much as it did the moment the Om reached his consciousness and he recognized his wretchedness and his crime.

'Om,' he pronounced inwardly, and he was conscious of Brahman, of the indestructibleness of life; he remembered all that he had forgotten, all that was divine.

But it was only for a moment, a flash. Siddhartha sank down at the foot of the coconut tree, overcome by fatigue. Murmuring Om, he laid his head on the tree roots and sank into a deep sleep.

His sleep was deep and dreamless; he had not slept like that for a long time. When he awakened after many hours, it seemed to him as if ten years had passed. He heard the soft rippling of the water; he did not know where he was nor what had brought him there. He looked up and was surprised to see the trees and the sky above him. He remembered where he was and how he came to be there. He felt a desire to remain there for a long time. The past now seemed to him to be covered by a veil, extremely remote, very unimportant. He only knew that his previous life (at the first moment of his return to consciousness his previous life seemed to him like a remote incarnation, like an earlier birth of his present Self) was finished, that it was so full of nausea and wretchedness that he had wanted to destroy it, but that he had come to himself by a river, under a coconut tree, with the holy word Om on his lips. Then he had fallen asleep, and on awakening he looked at the world like a new man. Softly he said the word Om to himself, over which he had fallen asleep, and it seemed to him as if his whole sleep had been a long deep pronouncing of Om, thinking of Om, an immersion and penetration into Om, into the nameless, into the Divine.

What a wonderful sleep it had been! Never had a sleep so refreshed him, so renewed him, so rejuvenated him! Perhaps he had really died, perhaps he had been drowned and was reborn in another form. No, he recognized himself, he recognized his hands and feet, the place where he lay and the Self in his breast, Siddhartha, self-willed, individualistic. But this Siddhartha was somewhat changed, renewed. He had slept wonderfully. He was remarkably awake, happy and curious.

Siddhartha raised himself and saw a monk in a yellow gown, with shaved head, sitting opposite him in the attitude of a thinker. He looked at the man, who had neither hair on his head nor a beard, and he had not looked at him long when he recognized in this monk Govinda, the friend of his youth, Govinda who had taken refuge in the Illustrious Buddha. Govinda had also aged, but he still showed the old characteristics in his face – eagerness, loyalty, curiosity, anxiety. But when Govinda, feeling his glance, raised his eyes and looked at him, Siddhartha saw that Govinda did not recognize him. Govinda was pleased to find him awake. Apparently he had sat there a long time waiting for him to awaken, although he did not know him.

'I was sleeping,' said Siddhartha. 'How did you come here?'

'You were sleeping,' answered Govinda, 'and it is not good to sleep in such places where there are often snakes and animals from the forest prowling about. I am one of the followers of the Illustrious Gotama, the Buddha of Sakyamuni, and I am on a pilgrimage with a number of our order. I saw you lying asleep in a dangerous place, so I tried to awaken you, and then as I saw you were sleeping very deeply, I remained behind my brothers and sat by you. Then it seems that I, who wanted to watch over you, fell asleep myself. Weariness overcame me and I kept my watch badly. But now you are awake, so I must go and overtake my brothers.'

'I thank you, Samana, for guarding my sleep. The followers of the Illustrious One are very kind, but now you may go on your way.'

'I am going. May you keep well.'

'I thank you, Samana.'

Govinda bowed and said 'Goodbye.'

'Goodbye, Govinda,' said Siddhartha.

The monk stood still.

'Excuse me, sir, how do you know my name?'

Thereupon Siddhartha laughed.

'I know you, Govinda, from your father's house and from the Brahmins' school, and from the sacrifices, and from our sojourn with the Samanas and from that hour in the grove of Jetavana when you swore allegiance to the Illustrious One.'

'You are Siddhartha,' cried Govinda aloud. 'Now I recognize you and do not understand why I did not recognize you immediately. Greetings, Siddhartha, it gives me great pleasure to see you again.'

'I am also pleased to see you again. You have watched over me during my sleep. I thank you once again, although I needed no guard. Where are you going, my friend?'

'I am not going anywhere. We monks are always on the way, except during the rainy season. We always move from place to place, live according to the rule, preach the gospel, collect alms and then move on. It is always the same. But where are you going, Siddhartha?'

Siddhartha said: 'It is the same with me as it is with

you, my friend. I am not going anywhere. I am only on the way. I am making a pilgrimage.'

Govinda said: 'You say you are making a pilgrimage and I believe you. But forgive me, Siddhartha, you do not look like a pilgrim. You are wearing the clothes of a rich man, you are wearing the shoes of a man of fashion, and your perfumed hair is not the hair of a pilgrim, it is not the hair of a Samana.'

'You have observed well, my friend; you see everything with your sharp eyes. But I did not tell you that I am a Samana. I said I was making a pilgrimage and that is true.'

'You are making a pilgrimage,' said Govinda, 'but few make a pilgrimage in such clothes, in such shoes and with such hair. I, who have been wandering for many years, have never seen such a pilgrim.'

'I believe you, Govinda. But today you have met such a pilgrim in such shoes and dress. Remember, my dear Govinda, the world of appearances is transitory, the style of our clothes and hair is extremely transitory. Our hair and our bodies are themselves transitory. You have observed correctly. I am wearing the clothes of a rich man, and I am wearing them because I have been a rich man, and I am wearing my hair like men of the world and fashion because I have been one of them.'

'And what are you now, Siddhartha?'

'I do not know; I know as little as you. I am on the way. I was a rich man, but I am no longer and what I will be tomorrow I do not know.'

'Have you lost your riches?'

'I have lost them, or they have lost me – I am not sure. The wheel of appearances revolves quickly, Govinda. Where is Siddhartha the Brahmin, where is Siddhartha the Samana, where is Siddhartha the rich man? The transitory soon changes, Govinda. You know that.'

For a long time Govinda looked doubtfully at the friend of his youth. Then he bowed to him, as one does to a man of rank, and went on his way.

Smiling, Siddhartha watched him go. He still loved him, this faithful anxious friend. And at that moment, in that splendid hour, after his wonderful sleep, permeated with Om, how could he help but love someone and something. That was just the magic that had happened to him during his sleep and the Om in him – he loved everything, he was full of joyous love towards everything that he saw. And it seemed to him that was just why he was previously so ill – because he could love nothing and nobody.

With a smile Siddhartha watched the departing monk. His sleep had strengthened him, but he suffered great hunger for he had not eaten for two days, and the time was long past when he could ward off hunger. Troubled, yet also with laughter, he recalled that time. He remembered that at that time he had boasted of three things to Kamala, three noble and invincible arts: fasting, waiting and thinking. These were his possessions, his power and strength, his firm staff. He had learned these three arts and nothing else during the diligent, assiduous years of his youth. Now he had lost them, he possessed none of them any more, neither fasting, nor waiting, nor thinking. He had exchanged them for the most wretched things, for the transitory, for the pleasures of the senses, for high living and riches. He had gone along a strange path. And now, it seemed that he had indeed become an ordinary person.

Siddhartha reflected on his state. He found it difficult to think; he really had no desire to, but he forced himself.

Now, he thought, that all these transitory things have slipped away from me again, I stand once more beneath the sun, as I once stood as a small child. Nothing is mine, I know nothing, I possess nothing, I have learned nothing. How strange it is! Now, when I am no longer young, when my hair is fast growing grey, when strength begins to diminish, now I am beginning again like a child. He had to smile again. Yes, his destiny was strange! He was going backwards, and now he again stood empty and naked and ignorant in the world. But he did not grieve about it; no, he even felt a great desire to laugh, to laugh at himself, to laugh at this strange foolish world!

Things are going backwards with you, he said to himself and laughed, and as he said it, his glance lighted on the river, and he saw the river also flowing continually backwards, singing merrily. That pleased him immensely; he smiled cheerfully at the river. Was this not the river in which he had once wished to drown himself – hundreds of years ago – or had he dreamt it?

How strange his life had been, he thought. He had

wandered along strange paths. As a boy I was occupied with the gods and sacrifices, as a youth with asceticism, with thinking and meditation. I was in search of Brahman and revered the eternal in Atman. As a young man I was attracted to expiation. I lived in the woods, suffered heat and cold. I learned to fast, I learned to conquer my body. I then discovered with wonder the teachings of the great Buddha. I felt knowledge and the unity of the world circulate in me like my own blood, but I also felt compelled to leave the Buddha and the great knowledge. I went and learned the pleasures of love from Kamala and business from Kamaswami. I hoarded money, I squandered money, I acquired a taste for rich food, I learned to stimulate my senses. I had to spend many years like that in order to lose my intelligence, to lose the power to think, to forget about the unity of things. Is it not true, that slowly and through many deviations I changed from a man into a child? From a thinker into an ordinary person? And yet this path has been good and the bird in my breast has not died. But what a path it has been! I have had to experience so much stupidity, so many vices, so much error, so much nausea, disillusionment and sorrow, just in order to become a child again and begin anew. But it was right that it should be so; my eyes and heart acclaim it. I had to experience despair, I had to sink to the greatest mental depths, to thoughts of suicide, in order to experience grace, to hear Om again, to sleep deeply again and to awaken refreshed again. I had to become a fool again in order to find

Atman in myself. I had to sin in order to live again. Whither will my path yet lead me? This path is stupid, it goes in spirals, perhaps in circles, but whichever way it goes, I will follow it.

He was aware of a great happiness mounting within him.

Where does it come from, he asked himself? What is the reason for this feeling of happiness? Does it arise from my good long sleep which has done me so much good? Or from the word Om which I pronounced? Or because I have run away, because my flight is accomplished, because I am at last free again and stand like a child beneath the sky? Ah, how good this flight has been, the liberation! In the place from which I escaped there was always an atmosphere of pomade, spice, excess and inertia. How I hated that world of riches, carousing and playing! How I hated myself for remaining so long in that horrible world! How I hated myself, thwarted, poisoned and tortured myself, made myself old and ugly. Never again, as I once fondly imagined, will I consider that Siddhartha is clever. But one thing I have done well, which pleases me, which I must praise – I have now put an end to that self-detestation, to that foolish empty life. I commend you, Siddhartha, that after so many years of folly, you have again had a good idea, that you have accomplished something, that you have again heard the bird in your breast sing and followed it.

So he praised himself, was pleased with himself and listened curiously to his stomach which rumbled from hunger. He felt he had thoroughly tasted and ejected a portion of sorrow, a portion of misery during those past times, that he had consumed them up to a point of despair and death. But all was well. He could have remained much longer with Kamaswami, made and squandered money, fed his body and neglected his soul; he could have dwelt for a long time yet in that soft, well-upholstered hell, if this had not happened, this moment of complete hopelessness and despair and the tense moment when he had bent over the flowing water, ready to commit suicide. This despair, this extreme nausea which he had experienced had not overpowered him. The bird, the clear spring and voice within him was still alive – that was why he rejoiced, that was why he laughed, that was why his face was radiant under his grey hair.

It is a good thing to experience everything oneself, he thought. As a child I learned that pleasures of the world and riches were not good. I have known it for a long time, but I have only just experienced it. Now I know it not only with my intellect, but with my eyes, with my heart, with my stomach. It is a good thing that I know this.

He thought long of the change in him, listened to the bird singing happily. If this bird within him had died, would he have perished? No, something else in him had died, something that he had long desired should perish. Was it not what he had once wished to destroy during his ardent years of asceticism? Was it not his Self, his small, fearful and proud Self, with which he had wrestled for so many years, but which had always conquered him again, which appeared each time again and again, which robbed him of happiness and filled him with fear? Was it not this which had finally died today in the wood by this delightful river? Was it not because of its death that he was now like a child, so full of trust and happiness, without fear?

Siddhartha now also realized why he had struggled in vain with this Self when he was a Brahmin and an ascetic. Too much knowledge had hindered him; too many holy verses, too many sacrificial rites, too much mortification of the flesh, too much doing and striving. He had been full of arrogance; he had always been the cleverest, the most eager – always a step ahead of the others, always the learned and intellectual one, always the priest or the sage. His Self had crawled into his priesthood, into his arrogance, into his intellectuality. It sat there tightly and grew, while he thought he was destroying it by fasting and penitence. Now he understood it and realized that the inward voice had been right, that no teacher could have brought him salvation. That was why he had to go into the world, to lose himself in power, women and money; that was why he had to be a merchant, a dice player, a drinker and a man of property, until the priest and Samana in him were dead. That was why he had to undergo those horrible years, suffer nausea, learn the lesson of the madness of an empty, futile life till the end, till he reached bitter despair, so that Siddhartha the pleasure-monger and Siddhartha the man of property could die.

He had died and a new Siddhartha had awakened from his sleep. He also would grow old and die. Siddhartha was transitory, all forms were transitory, but today he was young, he was a child – the new Siddhartha – and he was very happy.

These thoughts passed through his mind. Smiling, he listened to his stomach, listened thankfully to a humming bee. Happily he looked into the flowing river. Never had a river attracted him as much as this one. Never had he found the voice and appearance of flowing water so beautiful. It seemed to him as if the river had something special to tell him, something which he did not know, something which still awaited him. Siddhartha had wanted to drown himself in this river; the old, tired, despairing Siddhartha was today drowned in it. The new Siddhartha felt a deep love for this flowing water and decided that he would not leave it again so quickly.

The Ferryman

I will remain by this river, thought Siddhartha. It is the same river which I crossed on my way to the town. A friendly ferryman took me across. I will go to him. My path once led from his hut to a new life which is now old and dead. May my present path, my new life, start from there!

He looked lovingly into the flowing water, into the transparent green, into the crystal lines of its wonderful design. He saw bright pearls rise from the depths, bubbles swimming on the mirror, sky-blue reflected in them. The river looked at him with a thousand eyes – green, white, crystal, sky-blue. How he loved this river, how it enchanted him, how grateful he was to it! In his heart he heard the newly awakened voice speak, and it said to him: 'Love this river, stay by it, learn from it.' Yes, he wanted to learn from it, he wanted to listen to it. It seemed to him that whoever understood this river and its secrets would understand much more, many secrets, all secrets.

But today he only saw one of the river's secrets, one that gripped his soul. He saw that the water continually flowed and flowed and yet it was always there; it was always the same and yet every moment it was new.

Who could understand, conceive this? He did not understand it; he was only aware of a dim suspicion, a faint memory, divine voices.

Siddhartha rose; the pangs of hunger were becoming unbearable. He wandered painfully along the river bank, listened to the rippling of the water, listened to the gnawing hunger in his body.

When he reached the ferry the boat was already there and the ferryman, who had once taken the young Samana across, stood in the boat. Siddhartha recognized him again. He had also aged very much.

'Will you take me across?' he asked.

The ferryman, astonished to see such a distinguished-looking man alone and on foot, took him into the boat and set off.

'You have chosen a splendid life,' said Siddhartha. 'It must be fine to live near this river and sail on it every day.'

The rower smiled, swaying gently.

'It is fine, sir, as you say, but is not every life, every work fine?'

'Maybe, but I envy you yours.'

'Oh, you would soon lose your taste for it. It is not for people in fine clothes.'

Siddhartha laughed. 'I have already been judged by my clothes today and regarded with suspicion. Will you accept these clothes from me, which I find a nuisance? For I must tell you that I have no money to pay you for taking me across the river.'

'The gentleman is joking,' laughed the ferryman.

'I am not joking, my friend. You once previously took me across this river without payment, so please do it today also and take my clothes instead.'

'And will the gentleman continue without clothes?'

'I should prefer not to go farther. I should prefer it if you would give me some old clothes and keep me here as your assistant, or rather your apprentice, for I must learn how to handle the boat.'

The ferryman looked keenly at the stranger for a long time.

'I recognize you,' he said finally. 'You once slept in my hut. It is a long time ago, maybe more than twenty years ago. I took you across the river and we parted good friends. Were you not a Samana? I cannot remember your name.'

'My name is Siddhartha and I was a Samana when you last saw me.'

'You are welcome, Siddhartha. My name is Vasudeva. I hope you will be my guest today and also sleep in my hut, and tell me where you have come from and why you are so tired of your fine clothes.'

They had reached the middle of the river and Vasudeva rowed more strongly because of the current. He rowed calmly, with strong arms, watching the end of the boat.

Siddhartha sat and watched him and remembered how once, in those last Samana days, he had felt affection for this man. He gratefully accepted Vasudeva's invitation. When they reached the river bank, he helped him to secure the boat. Then Vasudeva led him into the hut, offered him bread and water, which Siddhartha ate with enjoyment, as well as the mango fruit which Vasudeva offered him.

Later, when the sun was beginning to set, they sat on a tree trunk by the river and Siddhartha told him about his origin and his life and how he had seen him today after that hour of despair. The story lasted late into the night.

Vasudeva listened with great attention; he heard all about his origin and childhood, about his studies, his seekings, his pleasures and needs. It was one of the ferryman's greatest virtues that, like few people, he knew how to listen. Without his saying a word, the speaker felt that Vasudeva took in every word, quietly, expectantly, that he missed nothing. He did not await anything with impatience and gave neither praise nor blame – he only listened. Siddhartha felt how wonderful it was to have such a listener who could be absorbed in his own life, his own strivings, his own sorrows.

However, towards the end of Siddhartha's story, when he told him about the tree by the river and his deep despair, about the holy Om, and how after his sleep he felt such a love for the river, the ferryman listened with doubled attention, completely absorbed, his eyes closed.

When Siddhartha had finished and there was a long pause, Vasudeva said: 'It is as I thought; the river has spoken to you. It is friendly towards you, too; it speaks to you. That is good, very good. Stay with me, Siddhartha, my friend. I once had a wife, her bed was at the side of mine, but she died long ago. I have lived alone for a long time. Come and live with me; there is room and food for both of us.'

'I thank you,' said Siddhartha, 'I thank you and accept. I also thank you, Vasudeva, for listening so well. There are few people who know how to listen and I have not met anybody who can do so like you. I will also learn from you in this respect.'

'You will learn it,' said Vasudeva, 'but not from me. The river has taught me to listen; you will learn from it, too. The river knows everything; one can learn everything from it. You have already learned from the river that it is good to strive downwards, to sink, to seek the depths. The rich and distinguished Siddhartha will become a rower; Siddhartha the learned Brahmin will become a ferryman. You have also learned this from the river. You will learn the other thing, too.'

After a long pause, Siddhartha said: 'What other thing, Vasudeva?'

Vasudeva rose. 'It has grown late,' he said, 'let us go to bed. I cannot tell you what the other thing is, my friend. You will find out, perhaps you already know. I am not a learned man; I do not know how to talk or think. I only know how to listen and be devout; otherwise I have learned nothing. If I could talk and teach, I would perhaps be a teacher, but as it is I am only a ferryman and it is my task to take people across this river. I have taken thousands of people across and to all of them my river has been nothing but a hindrance on their journey. They have travelled for money and business, to weddings and on pilgrimages; the river has been in their way and the ferryman was there to take them quickly across the obstacle. However, amongst the thousands there have been a few, four or five, to whom the river was not an obstacle. They have heard its voice and listened to it, and the river has become holy to them as it has to me. Let us now go to bed, Siddhartha.'

Siddhartha stayed with the ferryman and learned how to look after the boat, and when there was nothing to do at the ferry, he worked in the rice field with Vasudeva, gathered wood, and picked fruit from the banana trees. He learned how to make oars, how to improve the boat and to make baskets. He was pleased with everything that he did and learned and the days and months passed quickly. But he learned more from the river than Vasudeva could teach him. He learned from it continually. Above all, he learned from it how to listen, to listen with a still heart, with a waiting, open soul, without passion, without desire, without judgement, without opinions.

He lived happily with Vasudeva and occasionally they exchanged words, few and long-considered words. Vasudeva was no friend of words. Siddhartha was rarely successful in moving him to speak.

He once asked him, 'Have you also learned that secret from the river; that there is no such thing as time?'

A bright smile spread over Vasudeva's face.

'Yes, Siddhartha,' he said. 'Is this what you mean?

That the river is everywhere at the same time, at the source and at the mouth, at the waterfall, at the ferry, at the current, in the ocean and in the mountains, everywhere, and that the present only exists for it, not the shadow of the past, nor the shadow of the future?'

'That is it,' said Siddhartha, 'and when I learned that, I reviewed my life and it was also a river, and Siddhartha the boy, Siddhartha the mature man and Siddhartha the old man were only separated by shadows, not through reality. Siddhartha's previous lives were also not in the past, and his death and his return to Brahma are not in the future. Nothing was, nothing will be, everything has reality and presence.'

Siddhartha spoke with delight. This discovery had made him very happy. Was then not all sorrow in time, all self-torment and fear in time? Were not all difficulties and evil in the world conquered as soon as one conquered time, as soon as one dispelled time? He had spoken with delight, but Vasudeva just smiled radiantly at him and nodded his agreement. He stroked Siddhartha's shoulder and returned to his work.

And once again when the river swelled during the rainy season and roared loudly, Siddhartha said: 'Is it not true, my friend, that the river has very many voices? Has it not the voice of a king, of a warrior, of a bull, of a nightbird, of a pregnant woman and a sighing man, and a thousand other voices?'

'It is so,' nodded Vasudeva, 'the voices of all living creatures are in its voice.'

'And do you know,' continued Siddhartha, 'what

word it pronounces when one is successful in hearing all its ten thousand voices at the same time?'

Vasudeva laughed joyously; he bent towards Siddhartha and whispered the holy Om in his ear. And this was just what Siddhartha had heard.

As time went on his smile began to resemble the ferryman's, was almost equally radiant, almost equally full of happiness, equally lighting up through a thousand little wrinkles, equally childish, equally senile. Many travellers, when seeing both ferrymen together, took them for brothers. Often they sat together in the evening on the tree trunk by the river. They both listened silently to the water, which to them was not just water, but the voice of life, the voice of Being, of perpetual Becoming. And it sometimes happened that while listening to the river, they both thought the same thoughts, perhaps of a conversation of the previous day, or about one of the travellers whose fate and circumstances occupied their minds, or death, or their childhood; and when the river told them something good at the same moment, they looked at each other, both thinking the same thought, both happy at the same answer to the same question.

Something emanated from the ferry and from both ferrymen that many of the travellers felt. It sometimes happened that a traveller, after looking at the face of one of the ferrymen, began to talk about his life and troubles, confessed sins, asked for comfort and advice. It sometimes happened that someone would ask permission to spend an evening with them in order to

HERMANN HESSE

listen to the river. It also happened that curious people
came along, who had been told that two wise men,
magicians or holy men lived at the ferry. The curious
ones asked many questions but they received no replies,
and they found neither magicians nor wise men. They
only found two friendly old men, who appeared to be
mute, rather odd and stupid. And the curious ones
laughed and said how foolish and credible people were
to spread such wild rumours.

The years passed and nobody counted them. Then
one day, some monks came along, followers of Gotama,
the Buddha, and asked to be taken across the river. The
ferrymen learned from them that they were returning
to their great teacher as quickly as possible, for the
news had spread that the Illustrious One was seriously
ill and would soon suffer his last mortal death and
attain salvation. Not long afterwards another party of
monks arrived and then another, and the monks as well
as most of the other travellers talked of nothing but
Gotama and his approaching death. And as people
come from all sides to a military expedition or to the
crowning of a king, so did they gather together like
swarms of bees, drawn together by a magnet, to go
where the great Buddha was lying on his deathbed,
where this great event was taking place and where the
saviour of an age was passing into eternity.

Siddhartha thought a great deal at this time about
the dying sage whose voice had stirred thousands,
whose voice he had also once heard, whose holy countenance he had also once looked at with awe. He

thought lovingly of him, remembered his path to salvation and, smiling, remembered the words he had once uttered as a young man to the Illustrious One. It seemed to him that they had been arrogant and precocious words. For a long time he knew that he was not separated from Gotama, although he could not accept his teachings. No, a true seeker could not accept any teachings, not if he sincerely wished to find something. But he who had found could give his approval to every path, every goal; nothing separated him from all the other thousands who lived in eternity, who breathed the Divine.

One day, when very many people were making a pilgrimage to the dying Buddha, Kamala, once the most beautiful of courtesans, was also on her way. She had long retired from her previous way of life, had presented her garden to Gotama's monks, taking refuge in his teachings, and belonged to the women and benefactresses attached to the pilgrims. On hearing of Gotama's approaching death, she had set off on foot, wearing simple clothes, together with her son. They had reached the river on her way, but the boy soon became tired; he wanted to go home, he wanted to rest, he wanted to eat. He was often sulky and tearful. Kamala frequently had to rest with him. He was used to matching his will against hers. She had to feed him, comfort him, and scold him. He could not understand why his mother had to make this weary, miserable pilgrimage to an unknown place, to a strange man who was holy and was dying. Let him die – what did it matter to the boy?

The pilgrims were not far from Vasudeva's ferry, when little Siddhartha told his mother he wanted to rest. Kamala herself was tired, and while the boy ate a banana, she crouched down on the ground, half-closed her eyes and rested. Suddenly, however, she uttered a cry of pain. The boy, startled, looked at her and saw her face white with horror. From under her clothes a small black snake, which had bitten Kamala, crawled away.

They both ran on quickly in order to reach some people. When they were near the ferry, Kamala collapsed and could not go any farther. The boy cried out for help, meantime kissing and embracing his mother. She also joined in his loud cries, until the sounds reached Vasudeva, who was standing by the ferry. He came quickly, took the woman in his arms and carried her to the boat. The boy joined him and they soon arrived at the hut, where Siddhartha was standing and was just lighting the fire. He looked up and first saw the boy's face, which strangely reminded him of something. Then he saw Kamala, whom he recognized immediately, although she lay unconscious in the ferryman's arms. Then he knew that it was his own son whose face had so reminded him of something, and his heart beat quickly.

Kamala's wound was washed, but it was already black and her body had swelled. She was given a restorative and her consciousness returned. She was lying

176

on Siddhartha's bed in his hut and Siddhartha, whom she had once loved so much, was bending over her.

She thought she was dreaming and, smiling, she looked into her lover's face. Gradually, she realized her condition, remembered the bite and called anxiously for her son.

'Do not worry,' said Siddhartha, 'he is here.'

Kamala looked into his eyes. She found it difficult to speak with the poison in her system. 'You have grown old, my dear,' she said; 'you have become grey, but you are like the young Samana who once came to me in my garden, without clothes and with dusty feet. You are much more like him than when you left Kamaswami and me. Your eyes are like his, Siddhartha. Ah, I have also grown old, old – did you recognize me?'

Siddhartha smiled. 'I recognized you immediately, Kamala, my dear.'

Kamala indicated her son and said: 'Did you recognize him, too? He is your son.'

Her eyes wandered and closed. The boy began to cry. Siddhartha put him on his knee, let him weep and stroked his hair. Looking at the child's face, he remembered a Brahmin prayer which he had once learned when he himself was a small child. Slowly and in a singing voice he began to recite it; the words came back to him out of the past and his childhood. The child became quiet as he recited, still sobbed a little and then fell asleep. Siddhartha put him on Vasudeva's bed. Vasudeva stood by the hearth cooking rice. Siddhartha looked at him and Vasudeva smiled at him.

'She is dying,' said Siddhartha softly.

Vasudeva nodded. The firelight from the hearth was reflected in his kind face.

Kamala again regained consciousness. There was pain in her face; Siddhartha read the pain on her mouth, in her pallid face. He read it quietly, attentively, waiting, sharing her pain. Kamala was aware of this; her glance sought his.

Looking at him she said: 'Now I see that your eyes have also changed. They have become quite different. How do I recognize that you are still Siddhartha? You are Siddhartha and yet you are not like him.'

Siddhartha did not speak; silently he looked into her eyes.

'Have you attained it?' she asked. 'Have you found peace?'

He smiled and placed his hand on hers.

'Yes,' she said, 'I see it. I also will find peace.'

'You have found it,' whispered Siddhartha.

Kamala looked at him steadily. It had been her intention to make a pilgrimage to Gotama, to see the face of the Illustrious One, to obtain some of his peace, and instead she had only found him, and it was good, just as good as if she had seen the other. She wanted to tell him that, but her tongue no longer obeyed her will. Silently she looked at him and he saw the life fade from her eyes. When the last pain had filled and passed from her eyes, when the last shudder had passed through her body, his fingers closed her eyelids.

He sat there a long time looking at her dead face.

For a long time he looked at her mouth, her old tired mouth and her shrunken lips, and remembered how once, in the spring of his life, he had compared her lips with a freshly cut fig. For a long time he looked intently at the pale face, at the tired wrinkles and saw his own face like that, just as white, also dead, and at the same time he saw his face and hers, young, with red lips, with ardent eyes and he was overwhelmed with a feeling of the present and contemporary existence. In this hour he felt more acutely the indestructibleness of every life, the eternity of every moment.

When he rose, Vasudeva had prepared some rice for him, but Siddhartha did not eat. In the stable, where the goat was, the two old men straightened some straw and Vasudeva lay down. But Siddhartha went outside and sat in front of the hut all night, listening to the river, sunk in the past simultaneously affected and encompassed by all the periods of his life. From time to time, however, he rose, walked to the door of the hut and listened to hear if the boy were sleeping.

Early in the morning, before the sun was yet visible, Vasudeva came out of the stable and walked up to his friend.

'You have not slept,' he said.

'No, Vasudeva, I sat here and listened to the river. It has told me a great deal, it has filled me with many great thoughts, with thoughts of unity.'

'You have suffered, Siddhartha, yet I see that sadness has not entered your heart.'

'No, my dear friend. Why should I be sad? I who

was rich and happy have become still richer and happier. My son has been given to me.'

'I also welcome your son. But now, Siddhartha, let us go to work, there is much to be done. Kamala died on the same bed where my wife died. We shall also build Kamala's funeral pyre on the same hill where I once built my wife's funeral pyre.'

While the boy slept, they built a funeral pyre.

The Son

Frightened and weeping, the boy had attended his mother's burial; frightened and gloomy, he had listened to Siddhartha greeting him as his son and making him welcome in Vasudeva's hut. For days on end he sat with a pale face on the hill of the dead, looked away, locked his heart, fought and strove against his fate.

Siddhartha treated him with consideration and left him alone, for he respected his grief. Siddhartha understood that his son did not know him, that he could not love him as a father. Slowly, he also saw and realized that the eleven-year-old child was a spoilt mother's boy and had been brought up in the habits of the rich, that he was accustomed to fine food and a soft bed, accustomed to commanding servants. Siddhartha understood that the spoilt and grieving boy could not suddenly be content in a strange and poor place. He did not press him; he did a great deal for him and always saved the best morsels for him. Slowly, by friendly patience, he hoped to win him over.

He had considered himself rich and happy when the boy had come to him, but as time passed and the boy remained unfriendly and sulky, when he proved arrogant and defiant, when he would do no work, when he showed no respect to the old people and robbed Vasudeva's fruit trees, Siddhartha began to realize that no happiness and peace had come to him with his son, only sorrow and trouble. But he loved him and preferred the sorrow and trouble of his love rather than happiness and pleasure without the boy.

Since young Siddhartha was in the hut, the old men had shared the work. Vasudeva had taken over all the work at the ferry and Siddhartha, in order to be with his son, the work in the hut and the fields.

For many months Siddhartha waited patiently in the hope that his son would come to understand him, that he would accept his love and that he would perhaps return it. For many months Vasudeva observed this, waited and was silent. One day, when young Siddhartha was distressing his father with his defiance and temper and had broken both rice bowls, Vasudeva took his friend aside in the evening and talked to him.

'Forgive me,' he said. 'I am speaking to you as my friend. I can see that you are worried and unhappy. Your son, my dear friend, is troubling you, and also me. The young bird is accustomed to a different life, to a different nest. He did not run away from riches and the town with a feeling of nausea and disgust as you did; he has had to leave all these things against his will. I have asked the river, my friend, I have asked it many times, and the river laughed, it laughed at me and it laughed at you; it shook itself with laughter at our folly. Water will go to water, youth to youth. Your son will not be happy in this place. You ask the river and listen to what it says.'

Troubled, Siddhartha looked at the kind face, in which there were many good-natured wrinkles.

'How can I part from him?' he said softly. 'Give me time yet, my dear friend. I am fighting for him, I am trying to reach his heart. I will win him with love and patience. The river will also talk to him some day. He is also called.'

Vasudeva's smile became warmer. 'Oh yes,' he said, 'he is also called; he also belongs to the everlasting life. But do you and I know to what he is called, to which path, which deeds, which sorrows? His sorrows will not be slight. His heart is proud and hard. He will probably suffer much, make many mistakes, do much injustice and commit many sins. Tell me, my friend, are you educating your son? Is he obedient to you? Do you strike him or punish him?'

'No, Vasudeva, I do not do any of these things.'

'I knew it. You are not strict with him, you do not punish him, you do not command him – because you know that gentleness is stronger than severity, that water is stronger than rock, that love is stronger than force. Very good, I praise you. But is it not perhaps a mistake on your part not to be strict with him, not to punish him? Do you not chain him with your love? Do you not shame him daily with your goodness and patience and make it still more difficult for him? Do you not compel this arrogant, spoilt boy to live in a hut with two old banana eaters, to whom even rice is a dainty, whose thoughts cannot be the same as his, whose hearts are old and quiet and beat differently from his? Is he not constrained and punished by all this?'

Siddhartha looked at the ground in perplexity. 'What do you think I should do?' he asked softly.

Vasudeva said: 'Take him into the town; take him to his mother's house. There will be servants there; take him to them. And if they are no longer there, take him to a teacher, not just for the sake of education, but so that he can meet other boys and girls and be in the world to which he belongs. Have you never thought about it?'

'You can see into my heart,' said Siddhartha sadly. 'I have often thought about it. But how will he, who is so hard-hearted, go on in this world? Will he not consider himself superior, will he not lose himself in pleasure and power, will he not repeat all his father's mistakes, will he not perhaps be quite lost in Sansara?'

The ferryman smiled again. He touched Siddhartha's arm gently and said: 'Ask the river about it, my friend! Listen to it, laugh about it! Do you then really think that you have committed your follies in order to spare your son them? Can you then protect your son from Sansara? How? Through instruction, through prayers, through exhortation? My dear friend, have you forgotten that instructive story about Siddhartha, the Brahmin's son, which you once told me here? Who protected Siddhartha the Samana from Sansara, from sin, greed and folly? Could his father's piety, his teacher's exhortations, his own knowledge, his own seeking, protect him? Which father, which teacher, could prevent him from living his own life, from soiling himself with life, from loading himself with sin, from swallowing the bitter drink himself, from finding his own path? Do you think, my dear friend, that anybody is spared this path? Perhaps your little son, because you would like to see him spared sorrow and pain and disillusionment? But if you were to die ten times for him, you would not alter his destiny in the slightest.'

Never had Vasudeva talked so much. He thanked him in a friendly fashion, went troubled to his hut, but could not sleep. Vasudeva had not told him anything that he had not already thought and known himself. But stronger than his knowledge was his love for the boy, his devotion, his fear of losing him. Had he ever lost his heart to anybody so completely, had he ever loved anybody so much, so blindly, so painfully, so hopelessly and yet so happily?

Siddhartha could not take his friend's advice; he could not give up his son. He allowed the boy to command him, to be disrespectful to him. He was silent and waited; he began daily the mute battle of friendliness and patience. Vasudeva was also silent and waited, friendly, understanding, forbearing. They were both masters of patience.

Once, when the boy's face reminded him of Kamala, Siddhartha suddenly remembered something she had once said to him a long time ago. 'You cannot love,' she had said to him and he had agreed with her. He had compared himself with a star, and other people with falling leaves, and yet he had felt some reproach in her words. It was true that he had never fully lost himself in another person to such an extent as to forget himself; he had never undergone the follies of love for another person. He had never been able to do this, and it had then seemed to him that this was the biggest difference between him and the ordinary people. But now, since his son was there, he, Siddhartha, had become completely like one of the people, through sorrow, through loving. He was madly in love, a fool because of love. Now he also experienced belatedly, for once in his life, the strongest and strangest passion: he suffered tremendously through it and yet was uplifted, in some way renewed and richer.

He felt indeed that this love, this blind love for his son, was a very human passion, that it was Sansara, a troubled spring of deep water. At the same time he felt that it was not worthless, that it was necessary, that it came from his own nature. This emotion, this pain, these follies also had to be experienced.

In the meantime, his son let him commit his follies, let him strive, let him be humbled by his moods. There was nothing about his father that attracted him and nothing that he feared. This father was a good man, a kind gentle man, perhaps a pious man, perhaps a holy man – but all these were not qualities which could win the boy. This father who kept him in this wretched hut bored him, and when he answered his rudeness with a smile, every insult with friendliness, every naughtiness with kindness, that was the most hateful cunning of the old fox. The boy would have much preferred him to threaten him, to ill-treat him.

A day came when young Siddhartha said what was in his mind and openly turned against his father. The latter had told him to gather some twigs. But the boy did not leave the hut, he stood there, defiant and angry, stamped on the ground, clenched his fists and forcibly declared his hatred and contempt in his father's face.

'Bring your own twigs,' he shouted, foaming. 'I am not your servant. I know that you do not beat me; you dare not! I know, however, that you continually punish me and make me feel small with your piety and indulgence. You want me to become like, you, so pious, so gentle, so wise, but just to spite you, I would rather become a thief and a murderer and go to hell, than be like you. I hate you; you are not my father even if you have been my mother's lover a dozen times!'

Full of rage and misery, he found an outlet in a stream of wild and angry words at his father. Then the boy ran away and only returned late in the evening.

The following morning he had disappeared. A small two-coloured basket made of bast, in which the ferrymen kept the copper and silver coins which they received as their payment, had also disappeared. The boat, too, had gone. Siddhartha saw it on the other side of the bank. The boy had run away.

'I must follow him,' said Siddhartha, who had been in great distress since the boy's hard words of the previous day. 'A child cannot go through the forest alone;

he will come to some harm. We must make a raft, Vasudeva, in order to cross the river.'

'We will make a raft,' said Vasudeva, 'in order to fetch our boat which the boy took away. But let him go, my friend, he is not a child any more; he knows how to look after himself. He is seeking the way to the town and he is right. Do not forget that. He is doing what you yourself have neglected to do. He is looking after himself; he is going his own way. Oh, Siddhartha, I can see you are suffering, suffering pain over which one should laugh, over which you will soon laugh yourself.'

Siddhartha did not reply. He already held the hatchet in his hands and began to build a raft from bamboo and Vasudeva helped him to bind the cane together with grass rope. Then they sailed across, were driven far out, but directed the raft upstream to the other bank.

'Why have you brought the hatchet with you?' asked Siddhartha.

Vasudeva said: 'It is possible that the oar of our boat is lost.'

But Siddhartha knew what his friend was thinking – probably that the boy would have thrown the oar away or broken it out of revenge and to prevent them following him. And indeed, there was no longer an oar in the boat. Vasudeva indicated the bottom of the boat and smiled at his friend as if to say: Do you not see what your son wishes to say? Do you not see that he does not wish to be followed? But he did not say it in words and started to make a new oar. Siddhartha took leave of him to look for the boy. Vasudeva did not hinder him.

Siddhartha had been in the forest a long time when the thought occurred to him that his search was useless. Either, he thought, the boy had long ago left the wood and reached the town, or if he were still on the way, he would hide from the pursuer. And when he reflected further, he found that he was not troubled about his son, that inwardly he knew he had neither come to any harm nor was threatened with danger in the forest. Nevertheless, he went on steadily, no longer to save him, but with a desire perhaps to see him again, and he walked up to the outskirts of the town.

When he reached the wide road near the town, he stood still at the entrance to the beautiful pleasure garden that had once belonged to Kamala, where he had once seen her in a sedan chair for the first time. The past rose before his eyes. Once again he saw himself standing there, a young, bearded, naked Samana, his hair full of dust. Siddhartha stood there a long time and looked through the open gate into the garden. He saw monks walking about under the beautiful trees.

He stood there for a long time, thinking, seeing pictures, seeing the story of his life. He stood there a long time looking at the monks, saw in their place the young Siddhartha and Kamala walking beneath the tall trees. Clearly he saw himself attended by Kamala and receiving her first kiss. He saw how he had arrogantly and contemptuously looked back on his Samana days, how he had proudly and eagerly begun his worldly life. He saw Kamaswami, the servants, the banquets, the dice players, the musicians. He saw Kamala's songbird in its cage; he lived it all over again, breathed Sansara, was again old and tired, again felt nausea and the desire to die, again heard the holy Om.

After he had stood for a long time at the gate to the garden, Siddhartha realized that the desire that had driven him to this place was foolish, that he could not help his son, that he should not force himself on him. He felt a deep love for the runaway boy, like a wound, and yet felt at the same time that this wound was not intended to fester in him, but that it should heal.

Because the wound did not heal during that hour, he was sad. In place of the goal which had brought him here after his son, there was only emptiness. Sadly, he sat down. He felt something die in his heart; he saw no more happiness, no goal. He sat there depressed and waited. He had learned this from the river: to wait, to have patience, to listen. He sat and listened in the dusty road, listened to his heart which beat wearily and sadly and waited for a voice. He crouched there and listened for many hours, saw no more visions, sank into emptiness and let himself sink without seeing a way out. And when he felt the wound smarting, he whispered the word Om, filled himself with Om. The monks in the garden saw him and as he crouched there for many hours and the dust collected on his grey hairs, one of the monks came towards him and placed two bananas in front of him. The old man did not see him.

A hand touching his shoulder awakened him from his trance. He recognized this gentle, timid touch and recovered. He rose and greeted Vasudeva, who had followed him. When he saw Vasudeva's kind face, looked at his little laughter wrinkles, into his bright eyes, he smiled also. He now saw the bananas lying near him. He picked them up, gave one to the ferryman and ate the other. Then he went silently with Vasudeva through the wood again, back to the ferry. Neither spoke of what had happened, neither mentioned the boy's name, neither spoke of his flight, nor of the wound. Siddhartha went to his bed in the hut and when Vasudeva went to him after a time to offer him some coconut milk, he found him asleep.

Om

The wound smarted for a long time. Siddhartha took many travellers across the river who had a son or a daughter with them, and he could not see any of them without envying them, without thinking: So many people possess this very great happiness – why not I? Even wicked people, thieves and robbers, have children, love them and are loved by them, except me. So childishly and illogically did he now reason; so much had he become like the ordinary people.

He now regarded people in a different light from previously: not very clever, not very proud and therefore all the more warm, curious and sympathetic.

When he now took the usual kind of travellers across, businessmen, soldiers and women, they no longer seemed alien to him as they once did. He did not understand or share their thoughts and views, but he shared with them life's urges and desires. Although he had reached a high stage of self-discipline and bore his last wound well, he now felt as if these ordinary people were his brothers. Their vanities, desires and trivialities no longer seemed absurd to him; they had become understandable, lovable and even worthy of respect. There was the blind love of a mother for her child, the blind foolish pride of a fond father for his only son, the blind eager strivings of a young vain woman for ornament and the admiration of men. All these little simple, foolish, but tremendously strong, vital, passionate urges and desires no longer seemed trivial to Siddhartha. For their sake he saw people live and do great things, travel, conduct wars, suffer and endure immensely, and he loved them for it. He saw life, vitality, the indestructible and Brahman in all their desires and needs. These people were worthy of love and admiration in their blind loyalty, in their blind strength and tenacity. With the exception of one small thing, one tiny little thing, they lacked nothing that the sage and thinker had, and that was the consciousness of the unity of all life. And many a time Siddhartha even doubted whether this knowledge, this thought, was of such great value, whether it was not also perhaps the childish self-flattery of thinkers, who were perhaps only thinking children. The men of the world were equal to the thinkers in every other respect and were often superior to them, just as animals in their tenacious undeviating actions in cases of necessity may often seem superior to human beings.

Within Siddhartha there slowly grew and ripened the knowledge of what wisdom really was and the goal of his long seeking. It was nothing but a preparation of the soul, a capacity, a secret art of thinking, feeling and breathing thoughts of unity at every moment of life. This thought matured in him slowly, and it was reflected in Vasudeva's old childlike face: harmony, knowledge of the eternal perfection of the world, and unity.

But the wound still smarted. Siddhartha thought yearningly and bitterly about his son, nursed his love and feeling of tenderness for him, let the pain gnaw at him, underwent all the follies of love. The flame did not extinguish itself.

One day, when the wound was smarting terribly, Siddhartha rowed across the river, consumed by longing, and got out of the boat with the purpose of going to the town to seek his son. The river flowed softly and gently; it was in the dry season but its voice rang out strangely. It was laughing, it was distinctly laughing! The river was laughing clearly and merrily at the old ferryman. Siddhartha stood still; he bent over the water in order to hear better. He saw his face reflected in the quietly moving water, and there was something in this reflection that reminded him of something he had forgotten, and when he reflected on it, he remembered. His face resembled that of another person, whom he had once known and loved and even feared. It resembled the face of his father, the Brahmin. He remembered how once, as a youth, he had compelled his father to let him go and join the ascetics, how he had taken leave of him, how he had gone and never returned. Had not his father also suffered the same pain that he was now suffering for his son? Had not his father died long ago, alone, without having seen his son again? Did he not expect the same fate? Was it not a comedy, a strange and stupid thing, this repetition, this course of events in a fateful circle?

The river laughed. Yes, that was how it was. Everything that was not suffered to the end and finally concluded, recurred, and the same sorrows were undergone. Siddhartha climbed into the boat again and rowed back to the hut, thinking of his father, thinking of his son, laughed at by the river, in conflict with himself, verging on despair, and no less inclined to laugh aloud at himself and the whole world. The wound still smarted; he still rebelled against his fate. There was still no serenity and conquest of his suffering. Yet he was hopeful and when he returned to the hut he was filled with an unconquerable desire to confess to Vasudeva, to disclose everything, to tell everything to the man who knew the art of listening.

Vasudeva sat in the hut weaving a basket. He no longer worked the ferryboat; his eyes were becoming weak, also his arms and hands, but unchanged and radiant were the happiness and the serene well-being in his face.

Siddhartha sat down beside the old man and slowly began to speak. He told him now what he had never mentioned before, how he had gone to the town that time, of his smarting wound, of his envy at the sight of happy fathers, of his knowledge of the folly of such feelings, of his hopeless struggle with himself. He mentioned everything, he could tell him everything, even the most painful things; he could disclose everything. He displayed his wound, told him of his flight that day, how he had rowed across the river with the object of wandering into the town, and how the river had laughed.

As he went on speaking and Vasudeva listened to him with a serene face, Siddhartha was more keenly aware than ever of Vasudeva's attentiveness. He felt his troubles, his anxieties and his secret hopes flow across to him and then return again. Disclosing his wound to his listener was the same as bathing it in the river, until it became cool and one with the river. As he went on talking and confessing, Siddhartha felt more and more that this was no longer Vasudeva, no longer a man who was listening to him. He felt that this motionless listener was absorbing his confession as a tree absorbs the rain, that this motionless man was the river itself, that he was God Himself, that he was eternity itself. As Siddhartha stopped thinking about himself and his wound, this recognition of the change in Vasudeva possessed him, and the more he realized it, the less strange did he find it; the more did he realize that everything was natural and in order, that Vasudeva had long ago, almost always been like that, only he did not quite recognize it; indeed he himself was hardly different from him. He felt that he now regarded Vasudeva as the people regarded the gods and that this could not last. Inwardly, he began to take leave of Vasudeva. In the meantime he went on talking.

When he had finished talking, Vasudeva directed his somewhat weakened glance at him. He did not speak, but his face silently radiated love and serenity, understanding and knowledge. He took Siddhartha's hand, led him to the seat on the river bank, sat down beside him and smiled at the river.

'You have heard it laugh,' he said, 'but you have not heard everything. Let us listen; you will hear more.'

They listened. The many-voiced song of the river echoed softly. Siddhartha looked into the river and saw many pictures in the flowing water. He saw his father, lonely, mourning for his son; he saw himself, lonely, also with the bonds of longing for his faraway son; he saw his son, also lonely, the boy eagerly advancing along the burning path of life's desires, each one concentrating on his goal, each one obsessed by his goal, each one suffering. The river's voice was sorrowful. It sang with yearning and sadness, flowing towards its goal.

'Do you hear?' asked Vasudeva's mute glance. Siddhartha nodded.

'Listen better!' whispered Vasudeva.

Siddhartha tried to listen better. The picture of his father, his own picture, and the picture of his son all flowed into each other. Kamala's picture also appeared and flowed on, and the picture of Govinda and others emerged and passed on. They all became part of the river. It was the goal of all of them, yearning, desiring, suffering; and the river's voice was full of longing, full of smarting woe, full of insatiable desire. The river flowed on towards its goal. Siddhartha saw the river hasten, made up of himself and his relatives and all the people he had ever seen. All the waves and water hastened, suffering, towards goals, many goals, to the waterfall, to the sea, to the current, to the ocean and all goals were reached and each one was succeeded by another. The water changed to vapour and rose, became rain and came down again, became spring, brook and river, changed anew, flowed anew. But the yearning voice had altered. It still echoed sorrowfully, searchingly but other voices accompanied it, voices of pleasure and sorrow, good and evil voices, laughing and lamenting voices, hundreds of voices, thousands of voices.

Siddhartha listened. He was now listening intently, completely absorbed, quite empty, taking in everything. He felt that he had now completely learned the art of listening. He had often heard all this before, all these numerous voices in the river, but today they sounded different. He could no longer distinguish the different voices – the merry voice from the weeping voice, the childish voice from the manly voice. They all belonged to each other: the lament of those who yearn, the laughter of the wise, the cry of indignation and groan of the dying. They were all interwoven and interlocked, entwined in a thousand ways. And all the voices, all the goals, all the yearnings, all the sorrows, all the pleasures, all the good and evil, all of them together was the world. All of them together was the stream of events, the music of life.

When Siddhartha listened attentively to this river, to this song of a thousand voices; when he did not listen to the sorrow or laughter, when he did not bind his soul to any one particular voice and absorb it in his Self, but heard them all, the whole, the unity; then the great song of a thousand voices consisted of one word: Om – perfection.

'Do you hear?' asked Vasudeva's glance once again.

Vasudeva's smile was radiant; it hovered brightly in all the wrinkles of his old face, as the Om hovered over all the voices of the river. His smile was radiant as he looked at his friend, and now the same smile appeared on Siddhartha's face. His wound was healing, his pain was dispersing; his Self had merged into unity.

From that hour Siddhartha ceased to fight against his destiny. There shone in his face the serenity of knowledge, of one who is no longer confronted with conflict of desires, who has found salvation, who is in harmony with the stream of events, with the stream of life, full of sympathy and compassion, surrendering himself to the stream, belonging to the unity of all things.

As Vasudeva rose from the seat on the river bank, when he looked into Siddhartha's eyes and saw the serenity of knowledge shining in them, he touched his shoulder gently in his kind protective way and said: 'I have waited for this hour, my friend. Now it has arrived, let me go. I have been Vasudeva, the ferryman, for a long time. Now it is completed. Farewell hut, farewell river, farewell Siddhartha.'

Siddhartha bowed low before the departing man.

'I knew it,' he said softly. 'Are you going into the woods?'

'Yes, I am going into the woods: I am going into the unity of all things,' said Vasudeva, radiant.

And so he went away. Siddhartha watched him. With great joy and gravity he watched him, saw his steps full of peace, his face glowing, his form full of light.

Govinda

Govinda once spent a rest period with some other monks in the pleasure grove which Kamala, the courtesan, had once presented to the followers of Gotama. He heard talk of an old ferryman who lived by the river, a day's journey away, and whom many considered to be a sage. When Govinda moved on, he chose the path to the ferry, eager to see this ferryman, for although he had lived his life according to the rule and was also regarded with respect by the younger monks for his age and modesty, there was still restlessness in his heart and his seeking was unsatisfied.

He arrived at the river and asked the old man to take him across. When they climbed out of the boat on the other side, he said to the old man: 'You show much kindness to the monks and pilgrims; you have taken many of us across. Are you not also a seeker of the right path?'

There was a smile in Siddhartha's old eyes as he said: 'Do you call yourself a seeker, O venerable one, you who are already advanced in years and wear the robe of Gotama's monks?'

'I am indeed old,' said Govinda, 'but I have never ceased seeking. I will never cease seeking. That seems to be my destiny. It seems to me that you also have sought. Will you talk to me a little about it, my friend?'

Siddhartha said: 'What could I say to you that would be of value, except that perhaps you seek too much, that as a result of your seeking you cannot find.'

'How is that?' asked Govinda.

'When someone is seeking,' said Siddhartha, 'it happens quite easily that he only sees the thing that he is seeking; that he is unable to find anything, unable to absorb anything, because he is only thinking of the thing he is seeking, because he has a goal, because he is obsessed with his goal. Seeking means: to have a goal; but finding means: to be free, to be receptive, to have no goal. You, O worthy one, are perhaps indeed a seeker, for in striving towards your goal, you do not see many things that are under your nose.'

'I do not yet quite understand,' said Govinda. 'How do you mean?'

Siddhartha said: 'Once, O worthy one, many years ago, you came to this river and found a man sleeping there. You sat beside him to guard him while he slept, but you did not recognize the sleeping man, Govinda.'

Astonished and like one bewitched, the monk gazed at the ferryman.

'Are you Siddhartha?' he asked in a timid voice. 'I did not recognize you this time, too. I am very pleased to see you again, Siddhartha, very pleased. You have changed very much, my friend. And have you become a ferryman now?'

Siddhartha laughed warmly. 'Yes, I have become a

ferryman. Many people have to change a great deal and wear all sorts of clothes. I am one of those, my friend. You are very welcome, Govinda, and I invite you to stay the night in my hut.'

Govinda stayed the night in the hut and slept in the bed that had once been Vasudeva's. He asked the friend of his youth many questions and Siddhartha had a great deal to tell him about his life.

When it was time for Govinda to depart the following morning, he said with some hesitation: 'Before I go on my way, Siddhartha, I should like to ask you one more question. Have you a doctrine, belief or knowledge which you uphold, which helps you to live and do right?'

Siddhartha said: 'You know, my friend, that even as a young man, when we lived with the ascetics in the forest, I came to distrust doctrines and teachers and to turn my back on them. I am still of the same turn of mind, although I have, since that time, had many teachers. A beautiful courtesan was my teacher for a long time, and a rich merchant and a dice player. On one occasion, one of the Buddha's wandering monks was my teacher. He halted in his pilgrimage to sit beside me when I fell asleep in the forest. I also learned something from him and I am grateful to him, very grateful. But most of all, I have learned from this river and from my predecessor, Vasudeva. He was a simple man; he was not a thinker, but he realized the essential as well as Gotama. He was a holy man, a saint.'

Govinda said: 'It seems to me, Siddhartha, that you

still like to jest a little. I believe you and know that you have not followed any teacher, but have you not yourself, if not a doctrine, certain thoughts? Have you not discovered a certain knowledge yourself that has helped you to live? It would give me great pleasure if you would tell me something about this.'

Siddhartha said: 'Yes, I have had thoughts and knowledge here and there. Sometimes, for an hour or for a day, I have become aware of knowledge, just as one feels life in one's heart. I have had many thoughts, but it would be difficult for me to tell you about them. But this is one thought that has impressed me, Govinda. Wisdom is not communicable. The wisdom which a wise man tries to communicate always sounds foolish.'

'Are you jesting?' asked Govinda.

'No, I am telling you what I have discovered. Knowledge can be communicated, but not wisdom. One can find it, be fortified by it, do wonders through it, but one cannot communicate and teach it. I suspected this when I was still a youth and it was this that drove me away from teachers. There is one thought I have had, Govinda, which you will again think is a jest or folly: that is, in every truth the opposite is equally true. For example, a truth can only be expressed and enveloped in words if it is one-sided. Everything that is thought and expressed in words is one-sided, only half the truth; it all lacks totality, completeness, unity. When the Illustrious Buddha taught about the world, he had to divide it into Sansara and Nirvana, into illusion and truth, into suffering and salvation. One cannot do otherwise, there is no other method for those who teach. But the world itself, being in and around us, is never one-sided. Never is a man or a deed wholly Sansara or wholly Nirvana; never is a man wholly a saint or a sinner. This only seems so because we suffer the illusion that time is something real. Time is not real, Govinda. I have realized this repeatedly. And if time is not real, then the dividing line that seems to lie between this world and eternity, between suffering and bliss, between good and evil, is also an illusion.'

'How is that?' asked Govinda, puzzled.

'Listen, my friend! I am a sinner and you are a sinner, but some day the sinner will be Brahma again, will some day attain Nirvana, will some day become a Buddha. Now this "some day" is illusion; it is only a comparison. The sinner is not on the way to a Buddha-like state; he is not evolving, although our thinking cannot conceive things otherwise. No, the potential Buddha already exists in the sinner; his future is already there. The potential hidden Buddha must be recognized in him, in you, in everybody. The world, Govinda, is not imperfect or slowly evolving along a long path to perfection. No, it is perfect at every moment; every sin already carries grace within it, all small children are potential old men, all sucklings have death within them, all dying people – eternal life. It is not possible for one person to see how far another is on the way; the Buddha exists in the robber and dice player; the robber exists in the Brahmin. During deep meditation it is possible to dispel time, to see simultaneously all the past, present and future, and then everything is good, everything is perfect, everything is Brahman. Therefore, it seems to me that everything that exists is good – death as well as life, sin as well as holiness, wisdom as well as folly. Everything is necessary, everything needs only my agreement, my assent, my loving understanding; then all is well with me and nothing can harm me. I learned through my body and soul that it was necessary for me to sin, that I needed lust, that I had to strive for property and experience nausea and the depths of despair in order to learn not to resist them, in order to learn to love the world, and no longer compare it with some kind of desired imaginary world, some imaginary vision of perfection, but to leave it as it is, to love it and be glad to belong to it. These, Govinda, are some of the thoughts that are in my mind.'

Siddhartha bent down, lifted a stone from the ground and held it in his hand.

'This,' he said, handling it, 'is a stone, and within a certain length of time it will perhaps be soil and from the soil it will become plant, animal or man. Previously I should have said: This stone is just a stone; it has no value, it belongs to the world of Maya, but perhaps because within the cycle of change it can also become man and spirit, it is also of importance. That is what I should have thought. But now I think: This stone is stone; it is also animal, God and Buddha. I do not respect and love it because it was one thing and will become something else, but because it has already long been everything and always is everything. I love it just because it is a stone, because today and now it appears to me a stone. I see value and meaning in each one of its fine markings and cavities, in the yellow, in the grey, in the hardness and the sound of it when I knock it, in the dryness or dampness of its surface. There are stones that feel like oil or soap, that look like leaves or sand, and each one is different and worships Om in its own way; each one is Brahman. At the same time it is very much stone, oily or soapy, and that is just what pleases me and seems wonderful and worthy of worship. But I will say no more about it. Words do not express thoughts very well. They always become a little different immediately they are expressed, a little distorted, a little foolish. And yet it also pleases me and seems right that what is of value and wisdom to one man seems nonsense to another.'

Govinda had listened in silence.

'Why did you tell me about the stone?' he asked hesitatingly after a pause.

'I did so unintentionally. But perhaps it illustrates that I just love the stone and the river and all these things that we see and from which we can learn. I can love a stone, Govinda, and a tree or a piece of bark. These are things and one can love things. But one cannot love words. Therefore teachings are of no use to me; they have no hardness, no softness, no colours, no corners, no smell, no taste – they have nothing but words. Perhaps that is what prevents you from finding peace, perhaps there are too many words, for even salvation and virtue, Sansara and Nirvana are only words, Govinda. Nirvana is not a thing; there is only the word Nirvana.'

Govinda said 'Nirvana is not only a word, my friend; it is a thought.'

Siddhartha continued: 'It may be a thought, but I must confess, my friend, that I do not differentiate very much between thoughts and words. Quite frankly, I do not attach great importance to thoughts either. I attach more importance to things. For example, there was a man at this ferry who was my predecessor and teacher. He was a holy man who for many years believed only in the river and nothing else. He noticed that the river's voice spoke to him. He learned from it; it educated and taught him. The river seemed like a god to him and for many years he did not know that every wind, every cloud, every bird, every beetle is equally divine and knows and can teach just as well as the esteemed river. But when this holy man went off into the woods, he knew everything; he knew more than you and I, without teachers, without books, just because he believed in the river.'

Govinda said: 'But what you call thing, is it something real, something intrinsic? Is it not only the illusion of Maya, only image and appearance? Your stone, your tree, are they real?'

'This also does not trouble me much,' said Siddhartha. 'If they are illusion, then I also am illusion, and so they are always of the same nature as myself. It is that which makes them so lovable and venerable.

That is why I can love them. And here is a doctrine at which you will laugh. It seems to me, Govinda, that love is the most important thing in the world. It may be important to great thinkers to examine the world, to explain and despise it. But I think it is only important to love the world, not to despise it, not for us to hate each other, but to be able to regard the world and ourselves and all beings with love, admiration and respect.'

'I understand that,' said Govinda, 'but that is just what the Illustrious One called illusion. He preached benevolence, forbearance, sympathy, patience – but not love. He forbade us to bind ourselves to earthly love.'

'I know that,' said Siddhartha, smiling radiantly, 'I know that, Govinda, and here we find ourselves within the maze of meanings, within the conflict of words, for I will not deny that my words about love are in apparent contradiction to the teachings of Gotama. That is just why I distrust words so much, for I know that this contradiction is an illusion. I know that I am at one with Gotama. How, indeed, could he not know love, he who has recognized all humanity's vanity and tran-sitoriness, yet loves humanity so much that he has devoted a long life solely to help and teach people? Also with this great teacher, the thing to me is of greater importance than the words; his deeds and life are more important to me than his opinions. Not in speech or thought do I regard him as a great man, but in his deeds and life.'

The two old men were silent for a long time. Then

as Govinda was preparing to go, he said: 'I thank you, Siddhartha, for telling me something of your thoughts. Some of them are strange thoughts. I cannot grasp them all immediately. However, I thank you, and I wish you many peaceful days.'

Inwardly, however, he thought: Siddhartha is a strange man and he expresses strange thoughts. His ideas seem crazy. How different do the Illustrious One's doctrines sound! They are clear, straightforward, comprehensible; they contain nothing strange, wild or laughable. But Siddhartha's hands and feet, his eyes, his brow, his breathing, his smile, his greeting, his gait affect me differently from his thoughts. Never, since the time our Illustrious Gotama passed into Nirvana, have I ever met a man with the exception of Siddhartha about whom I felt: This is a holy man! His ideas may be strange, his words may sound foolish, but his glance and his hand, his skin and his hair, all radiate a purity, peace, serenity, gentleness and saintliness which I have never seen in any man since the recent death of our illustrious teacher.

While Govinda was thinking these thoughts and there was conflict in his heart, he again bowed to Siddhartha, full of affection towards him. He bowed low before the quietly seated man.

'Siddhartha,' he said, 'we are now old men. We may never see each other again in this life. I can see, my dear friend, that you have found peace. I realize that I have not found it. Tell me one more word, my esteemed friend, tell me something that I can conceive, something

I can understand! Give me something to help me on my way, Siddhartha. My path is often hard and dark.'

Siddhartha was silent and looked at him with his calm, peaceful smile. Govinda looked steadily in his face, with anxiety, with longing. Suffering, continual seeking and continual failure were written in his look.

Siddhartha saw it and smiled.

'Bend near to me!' he whispered in Govinda's ear. 'Come, still nearer, quite close! Kiss me on the forehead, Govinda.'

Although surprised, Govinda was compelled by a great love and presentiment to obey him; he leaned close to him and touched his forehead with his lips. As he did this, something wonderful happened to him. While he was still dwelling on Siddhartha's strange words, while he strove in vain to dispel the conception of time, to imagine Nirvana and Sansara as one, while even a certain contempt for his friend's words conflicted with a tremendous love and esteem for him, this happened to him.

He no longer saw the face of his friend Siddhartha. Instead he saw other faces, many faces, a long series, a continuous stream of faces – hundreds, thousands, which all came and disappeared and yet all seemed to be there at the same time, which all continually changed and renewed themselves and which were yet all Siddhartha. He saw the face of a fish, of a carp, with tremendous, painfully opened mouth, a dying fish with dimmed eyes. He saw the face of a newly born child, red and full of wrinkles, ready to cry. He saw the face of a murderer, saw him plunge a knife into the body of a man; at the same moment he saw this criminal kneeling down, bound, and his head cut off by an executioner. He saw the naked bodies of men and women in the postures and transports of passionate love. He saw corpses stretched out, still, cold, empty. He saw the heads of animals, boars, crocodiles, elephants, oxen, birds. He saw Krishna and Agni. He saw all these forms and faces in a thousand relationships to each other, all helping each other, loving, hating and destroying each other and become newly born. Each one was mortal, a passionate, painful example of all that is transitory. Yet none of them died, they only changed, were always reborn, continually had a new face: only time stood between one face and another. And all these forms and faces rested, flowed, reproduced, swam past and merged into each other, and over them all there was continually something thin, unreal and yet existing, stretched across like thin glass or ice, like a transparent skin, shell, form or mask of water – and this mask was Siddhartha's smiling face which Govinda touched with his lips at that moment. And Govinda saw that this mask-like smile, this smile of unity over the flowing forms, this smile of simultaneousness over the thousands of births and deaths – this smile of Siddhartha – was exactly the same as the calm, delicate, impenetrable, perhaps gracious, perhaps mocking, wise, thousand-fold smile of Gotama, the Buddha, as he had perceived it with awe a hundred times. It was in such a manner, Govinda knew, that the Perfect One smiled.

No longer knowing whether time existed, whether this uncovering had lasted a second or a hundred years, whether there was a Siddhartha, or a Gotama, a Self and others, wounded deeply by a divine arrow which gave him pleasure, deeply enchanted and exalted, Govinda stood yet a while bending over Siddhartha's peaceful face which he had just kissed, which had just been the stage of all present and future forms. His countenance was unchanged after the mirror of the thousand-fold forms had disappeared from the surface. He smiled peacefully and gently, perhaps very mockingly, exactly as the Illustrious One had smiled.

Govinda bowed low. Uncontrollable tears trickled down his old face. He was overwhelmed by a feeling of great love, of the most humble veneration. He bowed low, right down to the ground, in front of the man sitting there motionless, whose smile reminded him of everything that he had ever loved in his life, of everything that had ever been of value and holy in his life.